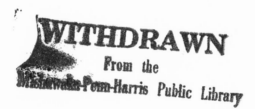

North Fork
to Hell

North Fork to Hell

DAN CUSHMAN

Sagebrush
Large Print Westerns

Library of Congress Cataloging-in-Publication Data

Cushman, Dan.
  North fork to hell / Dan Cushman.
  p.   cm.
  ISBN 1-57490-347-0 (lg. Print : alk. paper)
  1. Wyoming—Fiction. 2. Large type books. I. Title

PS3553.U738 N6 2001
813'.54—dc21   2001019042

Cataloguing in Publication Data is available from the British
Library and the National Library of Australia.

Sagebrush Large Print Westerns are published in the United
States and Canada by Thomas T. Beeler, Publisher, PO Box 659,
Hampton Falls, New Hampshire 03844-0659. ISBN 1-57490-347-0

Published in the United Kingdom, Eire, and the Republic of
South Africa by Isis Publishing Ltd, 7 Centremead, Osney
Mead, Oxford OX2 0ES England. ISBN 0-7531-6444-2

Published in Australia and New Zealand by Bolinda Publishing
Pty Ltd, 17 Mohr Street, Tullamarine, Victoria, Australia, 3043
ISBN 1-74030-301-6

Manufactured by Sheridan Books in Chelsea, Michigan.

North Fork to Hell

CHAPTER 1

THE STORM BLEW DOWN FROM CANADA, COVERING Montana territory with snow. The snow became sodden after passing the Yellowstone, and when it reached the North Platte it was a cold, slanting rain that mired wagons along the Oregon road. In the gold camps around Burnt Fork and Confederate east of the Rockies it was hoped that the storm would provide the runoff for a few weeks more sluicing, but freight outfits hauling supplies from Utah and San Francisco cursed it and hurried to make the deep coulee crossings before they filled with drifts ten feet deep. On the rivers a few laggard steamboats viewed it with hope and alarm, thankful for the last season rise which cold weather brought in its wake, but fearful of the freeze that might lock them in the ice of Dakotah.

It was a set snow which stuck to the skin, and made coatings across the north sides of the trees where it swirled around the Big Horns of northern Wyoming. In one of the precipitous coulees which ran down from a great hogback of that range, two white men had made a camp.

It was the sort of camp called a "wolf hole." The coulee, formed steplike from rapid erosion, had developed a number of hollows behind its spring waterfalls, and later, when it broadened and deepened, these became shallow caves high and dry along the sides. Occasionally one would form a small cavern under a projecting strata of sandrock, and become the den of coyotes, bobcats, or numerous smaller fauna. This one, however, was only a cup-shaped hollow with

1

a projection of shale to make a partial roof, and a frontal protection of chokecherry brush. Some of the larger chokecherries had been tied together and a couple of saddle-blankets tossed over to make a rude tepee. Smoke from a fire rose through the tepee and was quickly carried away by the wind. On a small bench below, three horses cropped the snow-clotted grass. Two of the horses were good saddle mounts showing the signs of hard travel. The third was a heavyset muley-horse with the hair marks and calluses left by packing gear.

The men drank tea and looked out at the storm. After finishing, and saving out the sodden leaves as a substitute for chewing tobacco, one of them put some black strips of buffalo jerky to boil on the coals and sat where he could watch the coulee, while the other curled up in some blankets on a heap of leaves in the back. The storm seemed endless, and the watcher dozed, but at times, after interminable periods of fifteen to thirty minutes, the wind would suddenly stop, leaving an alarming vacancy, and when this happened he would become alert and go outside for a look around. But each time there would be nothing. The country was desolate of movement. The horses, grazing, showed no nervousness as they might from a nearness of Indians.

He was a tall man with worn but expensive "Californy pants" which flapped in the wind around his lean legs. Each time, after looking, he would stamp around getting the circulation back, and then he would scratch himself, not just in the hairy places like someone with lice, but all over his body after the manner of one who had gone for days with his clothes on, filthy and not used to it. Then he would return to the fire.

On about his fifth trip his boot accidentally kicked the

jerky can, causing his companion to roll forward from his blankets as if propelled by springs, and he had a Colt Navy pistol in his hand. He remained crouched and blinking with the gun while the tall man laughed at him.

"Don't shoot, Doc. If I'd been a friendly Shoshone I'd be skinning your hair already."

"What was it?"

"Just me kicking the can around."

It was a mild joke. Up in the gold camps a man kicking the can around was having a spree. He had the slight, only slight, southern accent of one hailing from the Ohio River country. Or not the accent really, but rather a hesitancy in speaking, a good-humored slowness in saying even the simplest thing so it had the sound of maybe having a double meaning.

"God, I need a drink," said Doc. "I'm older than you are. I can't take this sort of thing. Listening to that wind . . . ! Every so often it has a howl like a Cherokee. It gives me the shakes."

He was shorter, heavier, and about ten years older than his companion, and he looked like somebody too much around liquor whose recent activities had caused him to lose about fifteen pounds of weight.

"Doc, that howl might be a Cheyenne, but you can bet it's no Cherokee. They're away to the south."

"I wish it was a Cherokee, then. We'd be out of this storm, maybe."

"Take a chew of this," he said offering him some of the sodden tea leaves. "Chinese chewing tobacco."

"Now, there's another thing! If a man could only have a chew or a smoke. You know, it's funny, one way of looking at it?"

"Tell me what way, Doc."

"Why, that stuff in there." He nudged the parfleche he

3

had been using as a pillow, and it resisted his toe with a heavy inertia. "Fifty pounds of gold! Eight-fifty fine! Best Montana color."

"The best Montana color is Bannack gold which I've seen run nine-ninety fine, which is a sight better than the U.S. government puts in its money. And there's no fifty pounds there, it's closer to forty-one."

"I was thinking while I was lying here how funny it would be if five-ten years from now, there we'd be dead, our bones washed away and everything, and this gold down the draw; well, somebody would find it and start the damnedest stampede you ever saw."

"Yes, that would be pretty funny."

They fell silent. The younger man looked at his watch and saw it was a quarter of twelve. The watch was a large one of heavy gold with a flip-open case engraved with hunters, dogs, and flying grouse. Inside was an inscription,

To Morgan McCoy
on his Twenty-first Birthday

He was very fond of the watch. His fondness for it had made him rather famous down in California. Some highwaymen had got him down from the Yuba stage, and he was willing to be robbed of his money, but when one of them attempted to take the watch, McCoy, without thinking too deeply about the consequences, had shot him dead with a ball from a double-Derringer which had escaped notice in his side vest pocket. That left the second barrel, and the three highwaymen still standing were presented with quite a problem. McCoy had only one more shot so he was no match for them, but which of them wanted to take that one shot? So they

4

reached sort of a silent agreement all around; they didn't do anything and he didn't do anything, and he kept the watch. So it won him something of a name. It also made him a man to be hunted out, it seemed, by every damn fool who wanted to win a gunman's reputation, and he had been forced to kill a man in Grass Valley, and finally—to escape a growing notoriety—to travel north to Fort Colville where he went into the freight business, to Okanagon where he ran for the Washington Legislature and was defeated by three votes, to the Beaverhead where he prospered as a ditch owner, to Tepee Gulch where he lost in a mining venture, and to Beartown, North Star and Sulphur City as a common stampeder, casebox keeper in a faro game, miner, surveyor, and recorder of claims. And finally, here he was, a fugitive.

It was as a recorder of claims that his present difficulty commenced. Two Ojibwas, scouts for the Mullen party who had built the famed road, by name Pete LeTurgey and Cross Guns, had turned up with a major discovery on what had been heretofore considered a barren piece of gravel, only to have their claims voted forfeit by the Sulphur Miners' Meeting. They were, it was pointed out by a loudmouth, name of Wickhorst, not only Indians but Canadian Indians—non-citizens by two counts. When McCoy rose to read from the law he was shouted down mainly by the Wickhorse crowd, threatened with violence, and called a Southern sympathizer in the recent war. This was not true, but he had run for the Washington Legislature on the Democratic ticket, so it looked bad for him. More important than the Indians' claims, however—their narrow but extremely rich paystreak having been mostly worked out—was the autumn cleanup which totaled

5

about 160 pounds, troy, in value about $33,000. The meeting declared this to be forfeit, but there arose a disagreement as to its disposal. Some were for dividing it on the spot. Others, however, pointed out that it should be divided only among the bona fide owners of claims along the gulch, and not split up with every Tom, Dick and Harry that happened to nose into the meeting. When this threatened to start a shooting fight, leaving out the very people who needed money the most, it was decided to place the gold "in escrow", which meant in the saloon strongbox at the Empire, the only iron-door safe in camp. So that night McCoy, and Doc Tiller, his present companion, entered masked and covered by blankets, herded eight late revelers into the cellar with shotguns, nailed down the trapdoor, and lifted the gold—quite a cargo—leaving the prisoners to their fate.

It had been their intention to keep only a fair commission for services rendered—25 percent was an amount mentioned—sending LeTurgey and Cross Guns away with the principal. However, a complication arose because McCoy had been recognized by his fine Spanish boots, and Tiller, until recently day bartender at the Empire, was strongly suspected for knowing the hiding place of the strongbox key. So they fled, split the gold into what each man could carry, the two Indians getting north to the Missouri River to lie low along the bank until one of the late steamboats picked them up; McCoy and Doc having a hot time of it, pursued by the Sulphur vigilantes—a group formed especially for their pursuit—and later by parties from Yellowstone City. There was little chance of being overtaken once they reached the roughlands of the Big Horns, but the northern tribes were nearly all on the prowl, raiding the roads to the gold camps; hence danger was far from past. They had traveled by night and slept by day, and neither had bathed or shaved in the last two weeks.

Doc got to his feet, head and shoulders bent under the roof-blanket, and looked at the storm. It closed off all view of the distances like fog. He shuddered and said, "God, I'm tired. I ache in every joint of my body. This cold . . . sleeping on the ground. It seems to rise up and set itself inside of you. It gets so it feels like a cold steel running down the marrow of your bones. You know, I'm not afraid of dying? When they practically had us up there in Yellowstone City I wasn't so scared. I thought, well, here it is. It's just that I don't want to die out here in this Godawful loneliness; I don't want to lie here forever and ever. This cold, and the wolves, and the snow drifting through my ribs . . . I know they say you don't feel anything after you're dead, but I don't want to die here."

"We'll get out, Doc." McCoy moved with sudden decision. "In fact we're going to start getting out of here right now, and daylight be damned. The Indians are all holed up someplace with this storm. We can saddle and drift ten miles before night with this wind at our tails. Ten times ten miles will take us to the North Fork, and another couple of days will put us in Soda Junction. Why, there might be a stage and we could go to South Pass City in style. Or Denver City. How does that strike you, Doc? Denver City!"

The coulee bottom was a series of grassy shelves through which the stream had made a new gash from two to ten feet deep. It descended in a series of steps where the horses had trouble with mud under the snow. Every quarter-mile or so the coulee would turn, and generally there would be some narrows with

7

perpendicular banks, and the men would follow the stream-bed where flat slabs of sandrock gave a clattering, treacherous footing covered with slush. After a while they were forced to hunt the broad bulge of the hill and run the greater risk of being seen, but the traveling was easier. The snow had been blown to a hard pack with grass showing through. The wind was at their backs. It kept the riders hunched forward with their coats pulled over their heads. In time the snow, thawing slightly as it struck, then freezing again, coated them thickly and froze to a clear ice over the horses' hindquarters.

They descended into a hummocky plain with the steep ridge of a hogback to the west. Much of the low area was shallow lake in the spring, and the snow had turned it to mud which lifted with the hoofs of the horses, making the going heavy, and leaving their tracks printed on the face of the land—black against white.

They rode on through little hills and came to a wide strip of horse tracks. McCoy got down for a close look, pronounced them mid-morning old.

"Cheyenne?"

"I'm not scout enough to know. But I don't believe this is Cheyenne country. These might be the friendly Shoshone."

It was a standard joke. The Shoshones, better known as the Snakes, had obtained numerous advantages through an official friendship with the whites but their war parties still roved, took scalps like the worst of the others.

Blowing loose snow down to where the impressions had frozen to a mud-ice, McCoy found that several of the horses were shod. "This is good old Eastern work-stock, some of it. Plenty of cleat on the shoes, too. It

8

was probably captured over on the Bozeman road. If so, these may be Arapahoes or Snakes headed back to winter quarters."

"How many do you think?"

"No way of telling. I'd say there were seventy or eighty horses, but how many have riders? Thirty? Just a guess, though."

Doc drew his repeating rifle from its scabbard. "That's a lot of Indians."

"Even after you shoot that Henry rifle dry it still leaves a lot of Indians."

"I know it sounds foolish, but it ain't being killed so much as the idea of being disemboweled and hacked to pieces that bothers me."

"And frozen."

"Yes, that too. Did I ever tell you I was with the freight outfit that came on the Mormons that were massacred down near Lemhi Creek? I don't like to think about it. It was too brutal and awful. They stripped 'em, and stuffed things in their mouths to give them the most awful expressions, and they cut all the men's dongs off."

"The squaws do that, Doc. This party is traveling too fast to have any squaws along."

"Why would they cut them off? Why would anybody do a thing like that?"

McCoy thought of a couple jokes he could make, but Doc was too upset, genuinely sick, and not at the thought of being killed, because he was no coward, but of being dismembered, left for the wolves—and in the cold.

"Imagine the women doing a thing like that. Do they just carry 'em away?"

"We're going to get out of here, Doc. Yes we are, and

9

all of a piece. This storm is the best thing that could have happened. I'm telling you, two weeks from now we'll be sitting around snug and warm in South Pass City, maybe even put up in that eight-room hotel they built down there. And we'll be laughing our heads off over this."

"You really think so?"

"I really do."

He remounted and they fell in along the trail left by the Indians. It was an old ruse, to leave a trail. Theoretically, in their strength, a large party wasn't cautious, while smaller parties, coming on their sign, would be dissuaded from following with hostile intentions.

The snow had almost stopped, then it came in waves again, in a ground blizzard which covered whole areas of the tracks, or carried the snow away leaving the bare ground with the tracks not depressions at all, but little hoof-size lumps of frozen snow. They rode for an hour with their heads down, siding to the storm, when of a sudden the wind paused, the snow whirled away, and with a muttered, "Good Lord!" McCoy drew up.

"What is it?"

"Look at the ridge."

There were horses just beneath the rock crest of a hogback. Men were crouched among the rocks. They were Indians. Something beyond held their attention.

"Easy!" said McCoy. "They see us. Sure they see us. But they think we're some of *theirs*!"

Doc had drawn his rifle. He levered it, forgetting there was already a cartridge in the chamber. The cartridge flipped out and left a hole in the snow. He fumbled and fed in another one.

"Wait!" said McCoy.

"I'm not doing anything. But by the God if they come for me I'll make a couple of 'em sorry."

"Sure you would." McCoy had seen him use the gun. He was a very good man with a gun. "Only we have to out-think 'em. White men are smarter than Indians. That's why the government takes care of them and never worries about us. The thing for us to do is act like *we are* Indians. Now, if we were Indians, what would we do?" He talked steadily to keep up his nerve and not bolt and run for it. "Why, we'd do what we are doing, just canter along like we were going to swing up to that ridge from the up-country side. Yonder's a draw. We'll ride into it, and they won't think too much about it when we just don't come right out again. God willing, there'll be some storm and there we'll be, headed south like this never happened."

The snow kept coming, but thinner, or it seemed thinner as they kept riding—riding and approaching one group of the Indians. These turned to look, but for the most part they were more intent on something at the far side.

"What do you suppose they're looking at?" asked McCoy.

"Maybe it's a wagon train."

"Not here. We're too far east for the Bridger road. They'd be penned between the canyon and the mountains."

"You could get through with a packtrain."

"It could be a packtrain. If a packer was crazy it could be. But my guess is they're Snakes watching Arapahoes, or vice versa. Or Crows, even Blackfeet. Even Cheyennes. All the tribes are stirred up with the railroad coming, and new roads pushing through everywhere to the gold camps. But that don't mean they've given off

11

killing one another."

They rode for a time in actual rifle-range, and could see the pinto, roan and bay colors of the waiting horses, even the flashes of red in the warriors' clothes; but none of them got up to mount, or gave a sign of suspicion, and finally the draw dipped down in front on them, and there was a welcome fringe of bushes.

"Cripes!" whispered Doc with the sound of a man who had been holding his breath for a long, long time.

There was a steep, sliding descent to a bottom filled with snow and rocks. It was narrow and twisting and brush choked the sides. The muley-horse gave trouble. After a quarter-mile it flattened out, the brush vanished, and they came out on an alluvial fan. This covered about forty acres and dropped down on an expanse of muck, ponds, and cattails. Fortunately the storm had increased. Behind them the ridge had become dim through the storm. Then they saw moving shapes— horsemen, Indians coming at an easy pace from the north.

An Indian in the lead saw them and came on tall and alert with a rifle in one hand. "Hay-ay!" he called.

"This is it!" said McCoy. "We got to ride for it."

As he spurred, a bullet flicked past. It stirred the air and was chased by the crack of explosion. Doc turned and fired. The lead Indian was unseated and half around on his horse. He tried to save himself and fell. The horse galloped on riderless. Other riders seemed scrambling and without purpose. Doc was at a good gallop, and had to check his horse and turn, waiting for McCoy who was having trouble with the muley. Luckily the ground blizzard was coming with dense ferocity, blotting out all the scene. They found themselves in marsh grass which made a frozen crunch under the hoofs.

"What are we getting into?" asked Doc.

"It's a slough."

The water lay in flat shining ponds an eighth- to a quarter-mile across. There was snow and ice around the edge. Some rushes grew farther out.

They had no choice but to keep going. Each of the ponds that made up the slough was ringed by grass which had stiffened with snow. It gave a precarious footing.

McCoy rode first, leading the muley. Doc, nervous with his rifle, followed. The Indians came on at a gallop and drew up at a lunging stop after two of their leaders rode belly-deep in water. There was some long-range shooting. A bullet glanced and plastered the belly of McCoy's horse with tar-black mud.

"To hell with that," he said to Doc, who was ready to commence levering the Henry dry in answer. "They're swinging around. We got to keep going."

They were about midway across, approximately 150 yards from either shore. The rim had made a wide swing and for many seconds, an interminable period, they seemed to be angling back with a loss of distance. No speed was possible. The footing was grass and moss growing on dead grass and moss which had stacked up over many years, and it trembled underfoot. There was tall grass with heads that looked like dried cauliflower.

A trio of ducks rose with a sudden pounding that frightened the horses more than gunfire. The muley lunged to the hips and fell and they were delayed in helping him. More bullets dug muddy foam. Ahead were cattails and shallow water. McCoy turned from the reef which seemed to wander nowhere and rode deeply through the rushes, a blessed concealment. He heard

13

Doc shoot twice with unknown effect. Answering bullets penetrated the cattails with sounds like ripping cloth. They climbed a muddy bank to solid earth and snow. Far away the Indians, shadowy through the storm, seemed to be milling without decision. One was waving a robe, evidently in signal to others beyond calling distance. Then several of the riders disengaged themselves from the group and started across.

"We can't let 'em do that," said Doc. "We got to make 'em go around."

"Well, I don't like it out here."

They rode on and found the natural breastworks of some dead cottonwood trunks at the edge of a flood-time gully. The gully provided protection for the horses, while the men dismounted for the knife-edge shooting and exact elevations necessary at long range.

"These are the real brave ones," said McCoy. "If we can slow these down, then it'll be time for the parliamentarians to take over. There's nobody that can argue and get nowhere like an Indian, and maybe we can make it to those little hills." He pulled out his watch. "It's four-forty already. There won't be enough light for a wolf to track us in this storm come six o'clock."

The Indians came singly: a vanguard of four, then a succession. Others waited their turn. Doc, after an impatient wait, squeezed the trigger.

The lead rider was smashed back across the rump of his horse as if struck by a crowbar. His horse was half-down and hip-deep, pawing wildly. There were answering shots, and the men back of the cottonwoods fired their guns empty and hot in their hands.

Riders were down and horses swimming. A lunging mixup had developed with some riders attempting to

14

press on and others to retreat. The leader, first hit, still had hold of his hackamore. It seemed to be wrapped around his wrist. He was dead and had the hackamore in a death grip. Every time the horse got footing and rose on the mucky reef, the weight of the man dragged him down again. But finally, backing away, he managed to strip the thongs over his ears and ran, promptly going to his belly in mire and slush.

"We better whop out of here," said McCoy. "We could shoot all day and not make a dent in them."

"I feel better. Those sons of bitches! Why'd they want to come for us? It wasn't as if we weren't trying to get out of their damn country."

"I know, but Indians are peculiar people. They don't just want the white man to leave, they want to scourge him out."

They mounted and rode as the storm and early twilight closed to make a gray-white endlessness. It became very quiet. The only sounds were of hoofs in snow and the creak of cold saddle-leather. The first of the little hills reared like ghosts through fog. Seeming high at first, on approaching they were scarcely hills at all, but only an intricate dissection by coulees and side gullies. The wind died out between the steep walls and the snow came down quietly.

McCoy rode and dozed. As it grew dark, he trusted the instinct of the big bay. He grew used to the sounds of its hoofs, and of the hoofs of the roan and the muley. He kept a certain posture because the snow kept settling on his shoulders and each time he turned some of it would sift down his neck. He lost all feeling of danger. Everything, all life but his own seemed to be shut out by the storm and the darkness. He might have been riding

15

for minutes or hours, when suddenly he was roused by something like a thunderclap of his nerves. He was alert and trying to see, hear, remember.

"Doc?" he said.

"Yah?" He roused sleepily.

"Did you hear anything?"

"No."

His horse was alert. That was it, there had been some hitch or hesitation. He sensed it now although it was so dark he could barely see the animal's ears ahead of him.

He reined in and Doc bumped him.

"What was it?"

He started to answer and suddenly there was a clatter of hoofs on stones, a startled Indian voice, and movement he could sense in the dark.

He said, "Indians!—we rode right into them—" and a gun cut him off, its flame seeming to burst directly in his face.

He drew and fired and Doc fired, and for a baffled moment they were caught in a blind, almost point-blank shootout. He turned around to retreat and was blocked by the muley-horse. Another horse was crowding past.

"Doc?" he said.

He realized at the same instant it wasn't Doc. It was one of the Indians. He turned in an attempt to bring his rifle up, but something hit him. He could not remember falling. He was on the ground. The thought came that he had been clubbed by the side of a steel-head lance, and the Indian above him was ready to run him through the chest.

Somehow he got hold of the stirrup. He held blindly as the horse dragged him. When he tried to get up the hoofs were cold chisels of iron, but he did not let go. He fell again and it was fortunate because his knee was on his rifle. He managed to pick up the rifle while holding the stirrup. One side of his head seemed to be gone. With the side of him still aware he heard riders and a final pair of shots.

Doc was calling and he couldn't answer.

"Morg? Where are you, Morg?"

He finally said, "Here!"

"Oh, I came near shooting you. Hey, what's the trouble?"

"I'm here. I got clubbed."

Doc got down to help him mount. His boot was so filled with snow it had to be shoved into the stirrup. His weight seemed at least five hundred pounds, and his leg dead to lifting. He pulled himself and finally belly-rolled to the saddle. The rifle was under one leg and it took all his strength to pull it out. He reached for the reins but he couldn't find them.

"I better tie you on."

"I'm all right. Where's the bridle?"

"I got it. Hey, you're bleeding all over hell."

"It's just a cut on my cheek." He held his kerchief over it. The kerchief, of black China-silk, was dense as a doctor's plaster. It smelled of smoke from use as a hot-can holder around the fire.

"You better hold some snow on it."

"No, I'm all right."

All he had to do was stay on the horse.

"Where are they?" he asked. "Where are those red sons-of-bitches now?"

"They got out of here. They thought we were ambushing *them*. The way you were pumping that rifle they thought you were the whole U.S. cavalry."

He found himself riding up a steep bank. The dirt rolled and he could smell wet clay, and dust. After a

17

struggle for footing the incline became less, there was snow, and grass under the snow, and the wind reached him like a hardened whip. It brought the first feeling back to the clubbed half of his face. By the glued-fast kerchief he knew that the bleeding was checked.

He rode, and after a while he experienced the strange sensation of having no horse or saddle under him. He found himself falling, but he couldn't fall. Someone had tied him by the saddle strings. It had to be Doc, of course. He had no recollection of Doc doing it. He kept sleeping and dreaming. It seemed that hours passed, more hours than in any single night, but it was still dark and snowing.

"How are you?" asked Doc, close against him.

"I'm all right. Where are we?"

"We're three or four miles north, out in the valley."

"North of what?"

"Of where we were."

"We've traveled all night."

"No, it's only been a couple of hours. Are you sure you're all right?"

"I think it broke my cheekbone." Every time he closed his jaw it felt as if his head were breaking in half right beneath the eyeballs.

"You need a drink?"

"What have you got?"

"Not what you need the worst, but I can dip you some of that slush-water. There's sort of a stream here."

He waited for it and drank from Doc's leather drinking cup. The water was very cold and it made his head ache. It caused a paralyzing pain to settle across his cheek and spread like a knife inward. He was thirsty, but he wanted no more to drink, he only wanted the pain to leave.

18

After a while he slept again, and next time when he awoke they were weaving through a rock field, along a steep sidehill, and then through the brush of a little, rock-choked draw. The wind hummed through the rocks, they were at the crest of the hogback, and he smelled woodsmoke.

He had had so many dreams that it seemed this was another, but he asked.

"Yah, it's smoke. There's a camp of some kind down there. I can see what's left of a couple fires."

"Indians?"

"I don't know. We'll have to chance it."

They rode steeply down and he dozed again. Suddenly he woke up at the sound of a voice. A shout, a curse!

"I said heave to!" a man cried.

"We're white. I got a wounded man here."

"What the hell you riding in this time a night for? Do you know I came almost giving you a blast of buckshot?"

"I didn't know we were so close."

"Get a look at 'em!" someone cried.

"Oh, hell, they're white men. Don't you think I can smell Injun?"

Then there were many voices, somebody called Denker, a man they called George, and a woman. The woman cursed like a man. The strings holding him were untied and he fell among arms that tried to support him. They cursed one another for letting him fall. He lay in the snow, and was helped to his feet, and he walked when they wanted him to walk. There were more people, wagons in the ruddy glow of campfires, and the hundred smells of a camp. Then he was able to lie full-length in a place that was warm and dry, and he did not

19

care if he died because he felt the strong contentment of being home.

He came awake by degrees, through a long period of half-dreaming, and then for a long time he lay on his back and looked at the gray light over him. There was canvas, and bows shaping it. From time to time he could hear the voices of men. They were Quaker-sounding voices but not Quaker exactly, either. It occurred to him that they might be Mormons and that would explain them being in such an out-of-the-way place, because Mormons set out to find new homes almost anywhere. He was in a wagon filled with boxes and bags, with space left for his bed, and room for a person to squeeze fore and aft. He started to sit up, became dizzy, and fell back. In doing it he made a sound and someone moved nearby. He sensed that it was a woman.

"Are you awake?" She had a young voice.

"Yes," he said, trying to turn.

"No, lie still. How are you?"

"I don't know. I took one alongside the head."

"Yes, I know. You were all blood."

"What is this, a wagon train?"

"Yes."

"Are you Mormons?"

"We are—most people call us Gileadeans."

"I was listening to voices outside."

"Yes, they were speaking with my father. He's Elder Hulbush. I am Bethel Hulbush."

"Let me see you."

She laughed and seemed pleased. He sensed that she was doing something, fixing her skirts perhaps, or her hair. Then she edged beside him in the close quarters. The hem of her long homespun overskirt brushed

20

against his shoulder. It was a plain habit topped by a coif shaped like a sliced-off stovepipe. The face under the coif was young and strong. It would be called pleasing rather than pretty. She smiled and it added color and warmth to everything.

"Are you hungry?" she asked.

"A little."

"You won't be able to chew. Brother Samuel thinks you have broken a bone."

"Don't go. Stay a while."

"We're getting ready to leave."

"Stay just a minute."

She remained and did little things about the bed. It gave him a feeling of security to see her, and feel her movements, and smell the sage- and soap-perfumes that came from her dress, the odors of laundry dried on sage clumps.

"I have to get it now. They always drink what soup is left just before setting out."

"All right."

The wagon seemed gray and cold without her. He could feel the seepage of air and knew it had settled into winter outside. By the stamping and link-chain sounds he knew the wagon was being hitched, and he was rocked by the geehaw of the team breaking the front wheels loose. He lay back with his eyes closed, waiting. Then he knew she was standing by his head again.

"Did I wake you up?"

The warm timbre of her voice made him think of Elissa, his aunt back in Ohio, his mother's much younger sister. He had always been secretly in love with Elissa.

"This isn't very warm." She held out a cup of soup.

"That's all right."

"You'll have to sit up. Can I help you?"

21

He got to his elbows with an effort, enduring the pain, and she rescued him with an arm under his back. She was wonderfully soft, warm, and strong. He tried to drink from the cup while she held it to his lips. It was a broth which seemed to have threads of turnips cooked up in it. He recognized them to be camas roots. He could not open his mouth wide enough. The liquid made him cough. He drank half the bowlful and could drink no more.

"Who is Elissa?" she asked.

It alarmed him. "When did I talk about Elissa?"

"Just as I came in. You called me Elissa."

He tried to recover from the fear of what he might have said in the delirium of the crazy, endless dreams of the past night. Once, years ago, when they were playing a game and he shared a hiding place with Elissa—one too crowded for them both—she had lain over him, and even yet, with startling reality, he could recall the structure of her body.

"Just now?"

"Yes."

"Is she your wife?"

"No, I'm unmarried."

"Sweetheart?"

"No. My aunt. You remind me of her."

She laughed.

"No, she's as young as you are . . . I mean, she was. When I saw her last."

They were shouting outside and there were sounds of other wagons. Then with a gigantic lurch their own wagon moved. After the first wave of dizziness it was not so bad. The movement went on steadily, deadening his senses. She talked and he did not answer. And he was aware of her hands fixing the bedclothes. He felt strangely secure, as if nothing truly bad could happen to him.

22

He awoke with the wagon hammering remorselessly under him.

"Bethel?" he asked, and got no answer.

He got up, enduring waves of black dizziness, and steadied himself against what seemed to be a knocked-down crated mill. He had rocking glimpses of the snow outside where the canvas failed to meet the wagon-box. There was a hilly skyline. The storm had lifted and there was some pale sunlight. It occurred to him that he had no idea where they were headed. After a time he saw by the afternoon shadows that they were headed north.

"Hello!" he said.

A gray-bearded man, beaten by work and weather until he was little more than skin over bones, bent to peer in at him. His cheeks were prominent because the skin had peeled, leaving them very red. He had rather wild-looking eyes. He wore black homespuns and a peculiar, round hat.

"Brother McCoy?"

"Yes."

"I am Elder Hulbush."

It was cold and McCoy stood barefoot in his long underwear. "Where are my clothes?"

"The women are mending them."

It was necessary to keep forcing his mind to make it work. One side of his head felt mashed and of no further use to him. This terrible thing had happened, and he had the feeling he would never be a whole man again.

"You better go back to bed, Brother."

"Where are we going?"

"Garden City."

"What?"

"Garden City."

"Montana?"

"Wyoming."

"I haven't heard of it."

"It's on the Big Horn River. Do you know Salmon Trout Creek and the Deepgrass Hills?"

"No."

"That is our goal. It's on the new road."

"You're not on a road." He could see no ruts, only the blankness preceding new tracks in snow.

"No, Brother. We are having a toilsome passage."

"You're going *north*!"

"Yes."

"Good God, this can't lead you to anywhere except the mountains. It will put you with the canyon on one side and the mountains on the other. Who's guiding you?"

"Major Garside is the commander. Our guide is Charles Denker. He is from Montana."

It seemed that he had heard of a Denker involved in . . . roads and wagons? trading? freight? It seemed to him that a Denker had been hanged up along the Missouri past Fort Benton.

"He's taking you north? Just *north*?" He couldn't acknowledge it. He felt that someone had to be misinformed. It had to be himself.

"We had to detour on account of the sandhills and the sloughs. We will cross the ridge soon and turn to Garden City southward and west. It will then be our task to build against the winter."

"This late?"

"We pray to have good weather yet."

"Yes, a few weeks, maybe. But this is Wyoming. It will be forty below zero. Indians. Game driven out of the country."

"It is our trial. We expected nothing easy."

"Denker?" He kept almost remembering the name.

"Yes, Brother."

"*Bigfoot* Denker?"

"Some call him that."

"A squawman."

"His wife is Indian. His son, Ignatius, is our scout. His daughter, Prairie Flower—he calls her Pet—she is with us also."

"It's his town? Garden City? I'd have heard of it."

"It takes people to make a town. When we arrive, build our houses, lay out our farms . . ."

His head was hammering. The voice was so sure and reasonable that it seemed that it had to be right and himself wrong, that there was a settlement named Garden City and they were rolling toward it. It was an attractive thought.

He slept and when he awoke the wagon had stopped. He got up and spoke without getting an answer. He looked out and saw that the train had paused at what was apparently a difficult creek crossing. Men were at the creek with extra mule teams on jerklines ready to help the heavily loaded wagons across. The wagon tops would drop almost from sight and rise again, pitching wildly as the teams dug in and they rolled up and over the far side. He could hear chickens cackling. The Gileadeans were distinguishable by their beards and round hats. There were other people dressed like ordinary wagon-emigrants, in catchall wool and felt.

He could recognize the Gileadean wagons because they were better kept, and their stock looked better. They used mostly mules, only a few horses, no oxen. Their cattle—he assumed it belonged to the Gileadeans by the round-hatted boys who tended the herd—was typical Eastern milkstock,

25

red-spotted, with some spring calves at their sides. The wagons and stock of the other emigrants, who formed a separate group, and even found a different creek crossing, looked extremely beaten-out. He saw Doc riding among the wagons. He had a new horse.

"Doc!" he tried to call, but shouting brought the paralyzing head pain back.

"How are you?" asked Bethel climbing to the seat and smiling in at him.

"Have you been driving?"

"Yes, Papa isn't too well."

"What the devil is 'Garden City'?"

"Nothing to do with the Devil."

"I'm sorry, but there's no such town. I've been trying to remember this fellow Denker. It's *Bigfoot* Denker. He had to get out of Montana. He was promoting a port on the Missouri River upstream from Fort Benton. He got a whole road crew massacred by the Bloods. Good God!" His head pounded and even with the wagon quiet he had to hold the sides. "It's coming on winter. It will be forty below zero. This country will freeze solid. You'll get down there on the Big Horn and find nothing. Nothing. Just . . . more of this. You'll survive in holes in the cutbanks. In another two months you'll be stripping bark from the cottonwoods to feed your mules. Your cattle will die. And the Indians . . . That's the heart of Snake country. And Bannacks . . . The Bannacks have been moving down from the gold country, driven out, massacred, their women . . . used. They'll be looking for revenge. They just want to kill, kill. Good God, to winter out in this awful alone . . ."

She climbed back from the seat looking frightened. Frightened, but for the wrong reason. Not because of his warning but because of him. He realized he must be

26

sounding wild and tried to become sure, positive, matter of fact.

"No, listen to me. You can't imagine how it will be. No game, nothing. No grass. The whole world just frozen. You'll be without fuel. You'll end by eating your mules." He saw Hulbush at the rear door. There were a couple of solid-looking Gileadean men with him. He turned to them. "Yes, and you'll end by eating one another! That's a terrible thing to say, but it's happened before and now is the time to say it. I know something about this country and its starvation winters."

"Brother McCoy," said Hulbush, "you have been sore beset by fever."

"Let me tell you . . ."

"We will give you your time to talk later. Your advice will be listened to. But you must go to bed now and rest."

"Come," said Bethel, her hand on him.

He had fever again and the fragments of dreams. Then he found himself sitting and drinking a bitter, warm draught which he recognized as willow-bark tea. He thought Bethel was driving, and yet she was holding him, protecting him from the lurch of the wagon.

"When you camp tonight will your people listen to me?" he asked.

"Yes," she said. "Of course they will. But you have to sleep now. Then Major Garside will see how you are."

"Is he a surgeon?"

"He is very good with wounded people. He was in the war."

"I'll be all right."

He was sure he would be all right as soon as the wagon stopped pounding, as soon as he could get as much as one hour of quiet.

He was awakened by a voice saying, "Get up! Get up and walk."

It was not a Gileadean voice. It was military, a voice of command.

"I'm Major Garside," he said. "I came to help you. Now, get up!"

McCoy was already on one knee. It was dark and someone was holding a light. It was a tin-can lantern with the door open, and he could see the smoky flame of a large, grease-dip candle. A man wearing mud-smeared boots was standing beside the lantern-holder. The boots looked huge. He was a big man, with powerful legs filling his trousers. The trousers were iron-tough whipcord with hunks of mud frozen to them. Major Garside.

He got up. The Major did not help him. Nobody helped him. He moved along, around the bed, down a passage crowded by bags and boxes. Major Garside followed him. The man with the lantern backed away and sprang to the ground.

"Catch him if he falls!" somebody said.

He nearly pitched face foremost into the dark, but he made a reflex grab, got hold of the rear doorway, and felt steps under him. He was barefoot and the steps were wet and cold. He went on, past people dimly lit by the lantern, and sank to his ankles in snow.

The Major said, "You see? He's as good as he has to be."

"Let him have his boots." That was Doc.

"They're in the wagon."

"Toss 'em down."

The boots almost hit him. He groped for them.

"No, let him put his boots on," said the Major. He came

28

and stood over McCoy. "Put your boots on!" he said.

He sat down on the rear steps and pulled on his boots. They went on hard over his snow-wet skin. Then he thought about his sox.

"Give me my sox," he managed to say with one half of his stiffened face.

A man laughed and said, "This fellow puts on his boots *first.*"

"Stop bullying him!" said Doc.

"What?" asked Major Garside.

"I said . . ."

"I heard what you said. Are you issuing the commands now?"

"I said to . . ."

Garside turned and hit him. It was a crashing blow, delivered short, but perfectly timed, set against the rising muscles of his legs. Doc went down. He landed in a half-sitting position, caught by his elbows.

"They don't argue with the Major," someone said.

Doc fumbled for his Navy revolver. Somebody kicked it out of its holster and away from his hand. He went crawling and groping for it.

"Let him have it," said Garside.

It struck McCoy that the Major wanted to shoot him. "No! No, Doc!"

But a blond young man picked up the Navy and kept it.

Garside said to Doc: "We saved you from the Indians. You needed us, but we don't need you. Any more trouble and you and your friend will be bullwhipped out of this camp, is that plain?"

"Don't argue!" said the young blond. He seemed to be a friend.

"All right," said Doc. "I won't argue."

The Major waited to make sure. He looked at Doc and

29

at McCoy. Then he gestured to McCoy. "Come here. I said come here, I want to have a look at your head."

He backed McCoy against one of the high, rear wagon wheels, clamped both hands around his skull, and held him up firm by a knee thrust in his crotch. "Bring the lantern! Get it up high. Higher. I want to see his eyeballs."

The light was in his eyes and McCoy was fixed by pain. He writhed to free himself, but Garside was bearing down with his hands.

"No," he heard the voice say. "No, there doesn't seem to be any bleeding of the brain. It'd show up in the eyeball. Get the lantern higher. There!"

Then he pressed and McCoy could see his face inches away. He was smiling and pressing with a power that seemed to be ripping his bones apart. McCoy fought, but he was helpless as a pinned fly and everything he did made the pain more terrible. Then he blacked out, and without a sensation of having fallen, came to on the ground.

He saw Garside's boots and trousers, his turned back, and heard him saying, "No, bandage be damned! He doesn't need a bandage. If he has any guts he'll get up and cure himself. If we wrap him in a bandage he'll never use the jaw again."

McCoy remained for a long time sitting with his legs thrust out, and his back against a wagon wheel. There were men nearby. He could see their shadows, their movements, and hear their muttering voices, but none were willing to give him a hand. It came to him that they were waiting for the Major to get out of sight.

"How are you?" someone asked.

He started to answer, and the pain stopped him. It gripped the entire right side of his head, and when he moved his jaw there was a grating and popping sound as if, under Major Garside's merciless hands, what had been a partial fracture was now broken apart, rocked and splintered, and rammed together again.

"Don't try to talk."

It started an argument. "He's got to use it," said Doc. "If he doesn't use it the bones will freeze and set that way."

Then as he sat holding his head, he heard another man tell something about an uncle who had gone to bed with a broken hip, and the one leg had thereupon proved useless and just withered away.

"McCoy! Mac!" It was the blond man—a giant in size—who had taken the gun from Doc. "Do you think you can get up and walk?"

He did not want anyone to touch him. He was willing to do anything for himself, just so nobody got near his tortured face.

"How about putting him back in the wagon?"

"No, that was the main trouble. Garside doesn't want him messing around with the Gileadeans."

"Especially the pretty ones, Halleck?"

It drew a cautious laugh.

"He doesn't want him stirring them all up with any more stories about Indians."

After Halleck was gone one of the men said, "That's why he ripped your head apart, McCoy. You were getting too close to that Hulbush girl."

"Don't make him talk, Aldo."

They made a bed for him under one of the wagons. By morning he had to get up and walk. A large, horsefaced woman fed him on mare's milk and corn gruel. She also held a mirror for him so he could see himself—face lopsided, one eye closed, a deep, red-swollen gash on his cheek running into a two weeks' growth of brown beard.

He started to say, "I was accounted a handsome man in my day," but he had to talk through his teeth and he gave it up. He made an attempt to smile.

"You'll be crooked-faced all your life, mister," she told him. "You got a bone splintered and mashed over. It ought to be cut open and scraped out, otherwise it'll cause the misery of hell before this winter is over."

Her husband said, "Those things should be left alone. If there's a bone to come out it'll work its own way. Like porcupine quills, arrowheads, anything else. They'll come out on their own if they're meant to come out."

The day passed. He endured it, and twilight came. The Gileadeans, who were somewhat in the lead, formed their own camp. The other emigrants, calling themselves Methodists as a means of distinction, camped in separate smaller groups, but within limits of the night patrol. Doc rode in from scout duty on a big-footed bay for which he had been made to trade. He told McCoy that Garside had forced him to pay one hundred dollars passage money, and he had given the Rimmel brothers twenty-five dollars for carrying their gear in the wagon. Aldo Rimmel was the blond giant of the night before. His brother Chuck looked like him but was darker. They were Pike's Peakers headed for the Montana gold fields via Garden City.

McCoy could not eat. He spent the next day unable to open his jaw more than enough to suck water through a reed. On the day following, weak from hunger, he ate by prying his teeth apart with a knife, and managed by painful repetition to get down a sort of gruel made of jerky, sent over from Denker's camp. Soon he was able to part his teeth a fraction of an inch without prying. He got over a perpetual dizziness and took his turn at driving.

The Rimmels had two jerry-wagons, light vehicles, hitched in tandem and pulled by a six-horse team. They also had an extra team, and a saddle horse which they took turns riding. It was their practice to keep the extra team in a jerkline harness, a very rudimentary affair which allowed them to graze and yet be ready to lend weight in the spots that were heavy going. Because of this, and the light wagons, the Rimmels' stock was in fairly good shape. Most of the emigrant stock seemed ready to fall. The Gileadean draft stock, as he had noted, were mostly mules, and their wagons were blacksmithed continuously along the way.

Major Garside owned a quantity of Army transport, also mule-pulled, and under the care of his own employees—single men for the most part, working their passage. There was also a saddle camp where the scouts and hunters, most of them half-breeds, lived a life of their own—a life of coming in after dark and leaving before dawn, and lantern-lit visits to the Major's commissary and munitions wagons.

The train moved northward, following the U of a wide valley, with the rocky summits of two hogback ridges closing them on the east and west. A pass supposedly broke the western ridge and was daily scouted by the half-breeds who used signal smokes, but to the slow-creeping train the ridge seemed endless. The snow stopped and it became warmer with the ground coming through and turning to mud. In such conditions their progress dropped from a maximum twelve to a heavy-wheeled five or six miles in a day. Continual patrol of Indians along the ridges forced the wagons to close in, nose-to-endgate and in double file, to prevent raids from cutting off segments for destruction. The feed was poor, and with no opportunity to drift and graze there was a growling bitterness among the "Methodists" that Garside was deliberately out to destroy them.

Chuck Rimmel said, "You see, those Mormons, or Holy Rollers, or whatever they are, have women and kids to gather hay right while they're going along. Besides, with good stock and wagons, they can always get out ahead for the first chance at it. That suits Garside, not only on account of him having his rope out for the Hulbush girl, but keeping us beat into line also. He wouldn't care if we all died except for needing us to fight the Snakes."

"He made Doc pay a hundred dollars for us," McCoy said.

"That's right. He charges fifty dollars for each man, and if you had a wagon he'd ask for fifty dollars more. We had to pay him two hundred dollars, and he thought he was being mighty generous to include blacksmithing and meat from the hunters. The only blacksmithing we had done was by one of those Holy Joes and he asked a dollar-fifty! And we haven't had a speck of meat since we left the sandhills."

"What *have* we been eating?"

"We have to buy it on the sly. There's a breed-kid comes in here at night sometimes with a haunch he hides from Garside and his so-called commissary."

"I'll pay my share."

"I'm not telling you on that account. I just want you to know how it stands with us. And with people like the Bowers, and Fisher, and Crane. They got kids and can't pay the damn hunters their dark-of-the-moon price. The Kavanaughs have got a sort of winery in their wagon and do better. However, the whole bunch of us would quit and head for Montana in a second if the time came.

The trouble is, none of us been north. We don't know the trails, crossing, anything. On the other hand, we don't dare approach that half-breed bunch because of Denker. He's in with the Major hand and glove. He's got a percentage. Furthermore, I'm not sure of it, but some of the boys claim Garside's been sleeping with Denker's daughter. She's that half-breed girl cooking for 'em." He grinned and added, "The one Doc has his eye on."

"Does Denker know about Garside?"

"Him sleeping with her? Oh, I suppose he does. You know how breeds and squawmen are. Just like a bunch of dogs. I suppose he thinks it might get him a few advantages."

The other Rimmel had ridden up beside them. He said to McCoy, "How about it, can you and your partner guide us back to Montana when it comes a chance for us to cut out?"

"I don't know that we could make it from this side of the river."

"You made it, didn't you?"

"Not with wagons."

"We'll take our chance."

"How about those other people? They willing to take a chance?"

"What are we taking anyhow, if not a chance? He'll see us all dead for the benefit of those Gileadeans."

Aldo said, "Benefit be damned. I sometimes wonder how *they'll* make out."

"Yes, but if half of them die this winter, what the hell?" said his brother. "As long as Garside has a permanent camp set up when the U.P. pushes through Wyoming next year, what does he care? Just so he's set solid in the swing position for any northern route up the Big Horn."

"How many will join you? *Positively.*"

35

Aldo said, "Well, we only got nine outfits for sure. Twenty-five people, seven of 'em women and kids. With you and Doc it makes twenty-seven. We might get more but we have to be pretty close-mouthed. If he ever got wind of it he'd come over here and shoot us. He wouldn't say a word—him and his private troops, they'd just open up."

McCoy laughed and felt his jaw. "How does he keep from being killed?"

"I'll tell you how. He does it by being one hell of a man. And he's one hell of a wagon captain. I won't deny that."

Chuck said, "How about it? Will you guide us north? We're willing to pay."

He smiled at the memory of Yellowstone City, and Sulphur, and what he had been running away from. Now they were asking him to go back, and putting it up to him in a way that was hard to refuse.

"I'd give you one chance in three of getting through this Indian country and the hogbacks and canyons to Montana. That is, with anything like your present outfits."

"We've talked about that and it's a chance we'll take."

Aldo said, "That's the truth, McCoy. We're going to make a break for it when the time comes, and whether you guide us or not."

"When do you think the time will come?"

"In about three days. That's supposed to put us at Primus Pass. It's an old fur trader's route down from the Big Horns. Cart route. Supposed to go over to the Bridger road."

Chuck added, "That's right, Morg. You got three days to decide whether you want to spit in the eye of Major Garside!"

The way he put it became a challenge.

36

CHAPTER 2

MAJOR HENRY BAUGH GARSIDE WAS THIRTY-SEVEN years old. He was intelligent, hard working and possessed of great physical distinction—even charm. He had few habits which the world called bad. He did not smoke, chew, drink, or even curse to excess. His life had fitted him for a hard struggle. Before reaching an age when he could cast his first vote for Franklin Pierce as fourteenth president of the United States he had been successively an orphan, a bound-boy on a Pennsylvania farm, a slate picker in a coal mine, apprentice to a wandering carriagemaker, deckhand on a Great Lakes paddlewheel steamboat, a company detective and a labor contractor. By the time he voted for Buchanan he had added the careers of independent warehouse-operator and colliery owner. During the early hard times of Buchanan's administration he became a bankrupt and a widower.

A month after his wife succumbed to tuberculosis Garside kicked a man to death in a quarrel over some driving harness. With a second wife, taken soon after the harness episode and already some months' pregnant, he moved to Leavenworth, Kansas, where he started a wheel-and-wagon manufactory. The enterprise failed. His infant son died of what was diagnosed as the milksick, and Garside, blaming his wife, moved into the cabin of a handsome octoroon girl down on the Lawrence Pike.

The war was just starting. Lincoln, then president, called for volunteers. Making arrangements for the octoroon girl to stay at a place called Frenchy's Free-Soil Ranche, a house of prostitution—and fifty dollars richer for it—

Garside returned to Illinois to enlist as a captain under Colonel G.M. Place, later Brigadier-General, a Springfield lawyer who had set out to gather a regiment which he called the First Illinois Rifles.

Garside quickly proved himself a competent officer, quick to make a decision which, once made, was ruthlessly carried out. His career was early clouded, however: as a disciplinary action, he once forced some insubordinate recruits to march twelve miles barefoot over a rocky railroad grade; one of them died of a gas-gangrene infection because he was too stupid to remove a fragment of gravel from a lacerated foot. Colonel Place hushed up the affair by promoting Garside to major and moving him to the command of a mule-depot in Hildiah. There misfortune continued to dog him, and he was broken to captain after the procurement scandals of 1863, serving the last months of the war as a transport officer. A belated recognition for his services came only after Major-General Custer was sent in June, 1865, to command the Department of Missouri. Custer decorated him for his part in the relief of the Third Wisconsin Cavalry at Fort Blair, Arkansas, and he was mustered out with the brevet rank of major.

Like many another veteran, Garside looked westward for opportunity. Investing in Army mules and rolling stock, in company with a cousin of his first wife, red-headed Dave Halleck, his faithful orderly, colored Abel Tunis, and a number of jobless men willing to work their passage, he set out for North Platte City, then end-of-line for the Union Pacific Railroad. It was Garside's speculation that a fortune might be realized there from a corral and wagon-repair works. However, his tenure in North Platte was complicated by a chance meeting, in one of the town's wood-and-canvas saloons, with a young Illinois veteran who had served under him in Missouri. The young veteran called him a son-of-a-bitch.

"If you would care to step outside with me?" Garside said.

He walked out in a military manner, the young veteran following, but on reaching the pole-sidewalk, turned unexpectedly and smashed him down with a left to the jaw. He had already lifted his Colt Navy revolver and had it under his jacket. It remained there while the young veteran, on his back and groggy, groped toward the butt of his own pistol. Killing him was almost too easy. As a nice touch, however, Garside placed the .36 caliber slug exactly in the center of his forehead. It was a very small round hole but the entire occipital portion of his skull was blown off.

"He drew his gun first," Garside addressed the crowd. "I call on every man as a witness that he drew first."

It was too obviously self-defense to call for more than a hurry-up glance from the marshal, hired by the saloon owners to keep all violence under the open sky outside. However, the young veteran had a number of friends, and Garside, never one to court trouble which had no element of personal gain—and having found the North Platte opportunities more meager than he had expected—set forth as master of a wagon train, ninety of whose 150-odd vehicles belonged to the members of an agricultural religious sect from Gilead, in southern Indiana.

It was the era of a thousand townsite promotions, and in the Gileadean group Garside recognized a valuable resource—the competent livestock- and tool-owning settlers who could make some town a going concern. He had an idea of taking them to Colorado where farm lands would be opened along the railroad mapped from

Denver north to the coming U.P. He fancied himself as their land agent, protector and supplier, and as their banker and middleman. He commenced carrying a Bible and was gratified when they called him "Brother Garside." He noticed Bethel Hulbush, the daughter of Elder Isaac Hulbush, dreamed of her as his wife, and took to having Abel Tunis prepare fresh rough-clothing each morning and fresh dress-clothing at suppertime each night.

He camped his train at Bear Meadows, South Crossing, Lebanon Graves, Staley's, and the Ash, choosing a slow but steady progress which saved the stock and met with favor from the Gileadeans. The range was poor. It had been dry that summer and the Indians, rising in their last great stand against the white invasion, kept every train narrowly to the traveled way.

At Brush Creek Crossing they came on an encampment of soldiers from Fort Hay burying the mutilated bodies of the Hubbard party. Later four members of that ill-fated group asked to join the train, and Garside took them at a lowered fee.

It was Garside's policy to extend credit to the wagoners wishing to join, but to accept only those with good livestock. Once on the trail he pressed them for money and in that way was able to take over a good horse or beef at an advantageous rate. It was this practice which led to the first real trouble on the train, and seemed for a while to endanger his position with the Gileadeans. He had demanded a fine bay horse from a Missourian named Griswold in foreclosure for a $35 debt, but later the man raised the amount and demanded the horse returned. Garside refused and Griswold, like the soldier at North Platte, called him a son-of-a-bitch. He felt he had no alternative but to shoot him dead on the spot. Griswold's twelve-year-old son Andy, hysterical and horrorstruck, tried to drag an old Jaeger rifle from the wagon, and Garside thought for a second he would have to kill the boy, too. Fortunately he hesitated until the last second; a man knocked the rifle from his hands, someone else clapped his foot on it, and he was able to stride away, turning his back with the contempt he had found to be so effective in the subordination of fractious recruits back in Missouri. Later he sent $100 to the widow. When it became apparent she was not going to refuse the money, the Major, laughing, said to Dave Halleck, "I shouldn't have sent her so much. The shortage of women being what it is, I endangered every husband in camp." A remark which Dave thought funny enough to retell all down that end of the train.

The Gileadeans had camped apart as usual, but the shot and the excitement had been heard, and that night Elder Hulbush offered his services at the funeral. He was refused because the deceased was a Methodist. For fear of an unfavorable distortion of the affair, Garside came around to Hulbush next day while his daughter, Bethel, a very handsome and full-blooming girl, was driving a second wagon at some distance.

"Brother Hulbush," said Garside, stripping his hat from his head and holding it with two hands across his breast, "you heard of the unfortunate affair with Griswold."

"I have not heard your story, Brother Garside."

He recounted briefly what had happened, saying merely that his leadership had been challenged, rather than repeating the offensive words "son-of-a-bitch," and Elder Hulbush grieved with him but accounted the affair unavoidable, and likened all emigrants to the children of Israel thrust into the wilderness. And he told about the

41

city Jericho whose walls were erected against them, and that Garside might take comfort from Joshua, and the words of the Lord Jehovah unto Joshua, "for the Lord had given over the silver and gold of that city to be consecrated into His hand, and also their vessels of brass and iron were consecrated unto the Lord, and it had come to pass that Jericho had stood against Joshua, so he had destroyed it, and all that was in that city, both men and women, young and old, and the ox, and sheep, and ass, he put to the edge of the sword. Hence it was that blood must run in the winning of a new country, for it was spoken, 'This is the land which I sware unto Abraham, unto Isaac, and unto Jacob, saying, I will give it unto thy seed.' "

Garside, keeping his horse at a jog, knowing he was handsome in his erect riding, and feeling the eyes of Bethel Hulbush on him, seemed to marvel at the words.

Major Garside had known many women, but until Bethel Hulbush, none but his first wife had touched him deeply. It was because he could not bear to see the fever-shine of life burn to extinction in her eyes that he had sought the comfort of the woman who became his second wife, and got her with child. And now, nine years after laying that poor girl away beneath the sad funeral bowers—he liked to remember the white-flowering spirea which was planted near her grave—Garside had found a woman who as peculiarly attracted him.

They were not in any manner alike, Bethel Hulbush and his first wife. Bethel had nothing of his first bride's delicate, ethereal manner. Yet he would ride for hours at some far edge of the dust-pouring wagons in order to watch her. Or stop when her wagon stopped to see her get down, and her strong young body move, the hint of healthy legs and hips under the rough, gray habit. Then at night he could not rest, but got up from his bed to walk among the Gileadeans' wagons, speak to the sentries, calling them "Brother Isaac," "Brother Zuph," or "Brother Samuel," as the case might be, until he was close to the wagon where *she* slept. He knew even where her bed was placed, and some nights he stood so close, with only the canvas between them, that he was aware of her quiet breathing, or a tremble of the wagon would tell him that she had turned in bed. Three nights after the shooting he stood so close he actually scented the odor of her body, and he felt the urge to climb the steps to her. But it was too risky. Everything, all his town-and-empire-building plans with the Gileadeans were at stake, ready to be imperiled if she cried out, and so he turned and hurried away. Later, with the desire for a woman mounting to anguish, he went to the Griswolds' wagon, the widow having accepted his $100 charity, and found her under a tent lean-to. Her protestations, negative and violent, were nonetheless whispered; she warned that her three sons, asleep elsewhere in the dark, might awaken, hence it was madness for him of all people to be there, but she finally relented for fear of the scene which would ensue if he were to be discovered. "Yes, yes, but be quiet, be quiet!" she whispered. Garside uttered not a word, pretending that the woman was Bethel.

"Ma, is that you?" one of the boys had asked, suddenly rousing.

"Yes, now go back to sleep. Go back to sleep!" she whispered fiercely. "Laws, child, it's nowheres *near* morning."

Next day the Major sent them a quantity of sugar, flour, and salt pork, and enjoyed the sense of being quite their benefactor.

All summer long the warlike tribes held the approaches to Colorado until that would-be state stood in virtual siege. Most of the freight companies considered the risk too great for even the 150 percent profit which was normal, but the wagons of the emigrants fought through by way of the South Platte. Yet in Colorado hard times lay across the camps, their gold running lean and their silver ores too refractory for the home-made charcoal furnaces. For every emigrant wagon getting through to Colorado, two of her own left for the north heading for the Montana gold fields. And eastward along the trail came word of the northern bonanzas. At Last Chance Gulch nine men were already rated as millionaires. The Diamond City stage station had a nabob's waiting room equipped with solid gold spittoons. There was a widow in Eldorado Gulch who took in washing and returned to her girlhood home in Iowa with the cash to purchase a small hotel, having recovered an average of $65 per day in gold from miners' clothes in the natural sluice of her laundry troughs. The Gileadeans, except for a couple of younger men, did not respond to the gold fever, averring that the Lord God Jehovah had intended them to farm, but even so they got a chuckle from the tale of a powerful tenderfoot named Ox Reedy who, at Top-o-Deep, near famed Beartown, attempted to lift a shovelful of "muck" and was chagrined to have his shovel break off in his hands, little realizing that it was almost pure "color" and weighed as much as a blacksmith's anvil!

In the region of Julesburg, with the news from Colorado becoming more hopeless by the day, Garside called a meeting and spoke briefly, setting forth the advantages to both farmers and miners, of the great, untouched lands which could be reached from the northern, or the old Oregon, route. The independents he did not worry about. Scarcely a wagon was not ready to cut out for the gold fields. It was a victory that the Gileadeans also decided to follow him. There was hardly a dissenting vote.

He turned north, crossing to the North Platte River, and through the late summer heat rolled into middle Wyoming. John Bozeman's road to the Montana gold fields turned off near the mouth of LaBonte Creek, a week after they left Fort Laramie. From a trading post and blacksmith shop newly erected one could look across the flats and cottonwood groves and see wagons and the dust of wagons and tent camps large and small where the emigrants waited—and attempted to organize into trains of the eighty-rifle strength the Army warned was necessary to repel Indian attack—and in the sunset of the flat horizon the dust of preceding wagons hung like a rusty fog.

It was not fear of Indians which dissuaded Garside from the Bozeman route, but the fact that it was drybone, a wolfhowl route which in winter would be locked in a cold like the Great Barrens and he now saw his main opportunity in commerce; for just as a railroad was to meet the U.P. from Denver in the south, so would lines tap the vast wealth of the north—its mines, farms, and forests.

Five wagons including a single apostate Gileadean left him for the Bozeman road. He picked up two other outfits however, and was able to leave behind the Griswolds—a relief, for the woman had become a nuisance, making almost nightly visits to his wagon. So she was left behind to argue with the blacksmith over repairs, and the train rolled on to Fort Casper, perhaps to there follow the

Bridger road northward along the Big Horn.

He supplied himself with Army maps at Caspar. Through inquiry he learned all he could of every road and trail. Bridger's road was beset by some rough canyon-going, but it promised the advantage of grass and water, and at least an imagined safety from the Cheyennes who were said to avoid the Big Horn—that area being solidly in the hands of the friendly Crows and Shoshones.

They traveled, holding the Bridger route as a possibility, while passing its main turn off, and every night there were meetings, particularly among independent wagoners. A great many wanted to break away and turn northward on their own, because the route Garside was following could only take them to the South Pass, and then it was either Utah or Idaho.

The final turn off to Bridger's road, or any road to the north, was at Fort Crook and the town of Soda Junction. There at last Garside had to make his decision, and there, providentially, he was presented with the opportunity he had dreamed of. It involved a townsite owned by a man named Denker . . .

It was September by the calendar, and mid-summer hot. But the sun set, and suddenly it was cold. It reminded one that Soda Junction was more than a mile in altitude—5,453 feet exactly by the geodetic readings. Wagoners who had been sweating with their shirts off, greasing and repairing their jacked-up vehicles, found themselves shivering when they bathed in the waters of Soda Creek, and the troopers from the fort were prone to stop cursing their government-issue blue wool tunics.

Garside, who had spent most of the afternoon among the officers at Fort Crook, was driven to town by a young trooper in the Colonel's converted ambulance-wagon. It was a shabby excuse of a town—a few log false-fronted buildings, some corrals, outlying shacks and half-dugouts, a street with ashes and bottles. Some Arapahoes camped using discard canvas rather than buffalo hides for their tepees.

"That's his place, right over there," the trooper said, pointing toward a shack in the outskirts. "The one with the tent behind. He lives there with his wife and six kids. She's a squaw."

"How about that oldest daughter? Is she a squaw, too?"

The trooper was stumped. "I don't know, sir."

"She's a half-breed?"

"Yes, sir."

"Pretty?"

"Yes, sir." He was uncomfortable and wanted to answer the right thing.

"Does she entertain the fellows from the fort?"

"What do you mean, sir?"

"You know what I mean, soldier!"

"She doesn't entertain them, sir. I understand she's decent."

Garside laughed. He bit off the end of a cigar and lit it. Gripping the cigar, his teeth looked powerful, and his eyes narrowed against the smoke.

"Is that the difference between a squaw and a half-breed girl?" he asked. "Does a squaw sleep with a soldier and a half-breed girl not?"

"I don't know. I hadn't thought about it, sir."

Garside grew tired of talking, got down, and stood with his back against a cottonwood tree, arms folded, watching the street. He smoked slowly, pausing at intervals to knock the ash from his cigar, doing it with his small finger which wore a snake-and-ruby ring.

"Sir!"

"Yes."

"That's him. Denker."

Denker was slouching and heavy booted. His face was thickly covered by black whiskers. He wore a black hat, and even from that distance one could tell he was filthy.

"Dirty Denker."

"Well, they call him that, too." And the trooper added to be helpful, "Don't lend him any money, sir."

Garside turned and looked at him.

"I only meant . . ."

"Wait for me here!"

"Yes, sir."

Dropping his cigar and grinding it into the dirt so its butt wouldn't be the slightest bit useful to the scavenger Indians, he crossed and followed Denker inside a saloon.

It was a deep hole of a place which managed to have a stale smell despite the illimitable winds of Wyoming. A boy was going around lighting lamps and setting them up in brackets. The lamps burned an oil sharpened by turpentine. A tall man with agate eyes, a dirty but tidy suit with a double-breasted vest, and an ornate watch charm was sitting on a stool behind a slotted table playing solitaire. He looked at Garside when he entered, but went on playing when he walked to the bar. There were half a dozen customers, all townspeople or wagoners—no soldiers. A soldier had been killed in a shooting scrape, shot down without a chance so the story went, and Colonel McNeel over at the fort was teaching the Junction saloonkeepers a lesson by declaring their places off limits.

48

Charlie Denker was waiting for service and being ignored by the owner, a good-looking young Irishman, and when Garside walked to the end of the bar he still ignored Denker and came over to ask his pleasure. The Major ordered bottled whisky, and after he had poured, and paid, the Irishman finally approached Denker. They immediately engaged in an altercation. Denker, it seemed, owed money, but there was some matter of a fat antelope-haunch delivered to the Irishman's home. After a while Denker became loud and bellicose. He was armed—there was a heavy double pistol thrust in the sash that held up his grease-slick black trousers—but he kept his hands in sight and a whining quality served to make his worst utterances not quite fighting words.

The proprietor said, "Denker, you want me to wipe the slate clean. Very well. Only get out of my place and stay out of my place. Do me that favor and, I'll call it even."

Denker did not move. He had another proposition, and he tried to talk about it in confidence.

"No," said the proprietor, "I've had enough of your schemes, your town lots, and your promissories. Money talks. In the future you enter this establishment on a cash basis."

Denker then paid for a whisky, filled his glass so full that surface tension actually made the brown liquid tremble over the rim, and balanced it to his lips. He ordered a second, truculently paid, and allowed it to stand there. Then he looked around and his eyes rested on the Major.

Although it was Denker he had come to see, Garside looked through him and beyond him with a gaze as unfriendly as the edge of a bowie. He had a sure sense of people, he could judge men as some men could judge horses, and he knew it would be wrong if Denker were to approach *him*. It would have to be the other way around. He wanted to be the man who acted, not reacted. It might have great bearing on everything that was to follow.

Denker, after his second whisky, began arguing with some teamsters. He claimed to have the power of predicting the sex of a foal three months before birth, and offered to bet on it. There was no way of settling the argument, so he then claimed he could guess the height of a certain hitching-post closer than any man in the house.

"Why, you Goddam old cheat, that post has been worth a hundred dollars to you this year," one of them said. Denker was unruffled. He did not mind being called the names, or later being asked about prairie-dog stew, a reference to his being a squawman.

When nobody would bet with him, Denker commenced to play blackjack "head-and-head" with the dealer. He lost and became surly.

"I wish he'd stay out of this place," the Irishman said, stopping across the bar from Garside. "You can't insult him. He'd have been killed a dozen times, but you could spit in his face and he wouldn't pull that gun."

"Why does he carry it?"

"That's just the point. He'd kill you, if things came up right, but he wouldn't fight if you spit in his face. What do you do with a man like that?"

"Is he a freighter?"

"No. He puts himself forward as a guide, claiming to have mapped the greatest of routes to the Montana gold fields, with a city, no less, midway along the route! A corral and a tin-cup saloon, I suppose—if even that. But his town plat makes it a veritable Dublin out in the desert, with streets, parks, watering troughs, everything."

The Major knew from his conversation with Colonel McNeel at the fort that he had a city platted up on the Lodgepole Meadows, halfway to the Yellowstone; that his "road" was the old Lodgepole Creek trail first followed by the Spaniards, running roughly between the Bozeman and Bridger routes until it joined Bridger's road near the Montana boundary; and that he had been petitioning the Army to set up a fort for protection near its southern end at North Fork.

"I have some of his corporate stock in settlement for debt," said the proprietor. "Everybody in town gave him credit on it, and I imagine also in South Pass City before he came here. Also I'm saddled with his town lots. I own two lots, one business and one residential. The business lot is next to the corner of Fifth and Main, and the residential is in what he calls Belle Vista. Crossen, at the store, has one lot he traded for five pounds of tobacco. Ninety cents a pound, four dollars and fifty cents, total. I ask you, what kind of a town is it with lots for four-fifty?"

Denker was arguing. In a braying voice he insisted that the dealer accept "table stakes" which in this instance included a counterfeit dollar. He said he had in fact received the dollar from him only yesterday. When the dealer refused to talk about it, Denker said he would recommend that people not play this table any more. But he went on playing himself.

"He'd better be careful," the proprietor said. "That's Jim Freeze. He won't put up with it like most of us do. He killed a man down in Colorado."

Surely and rheumy-eyed, Denker put out a Mexican dollar, which he pointed out was worth a dollar and ten cents. Freeze acceded to this, showing Mexican money

51

in his pay drawer. Denker won and called for whisky. The proprietor refused to bring it to him. Denker insisted, and finally one of the teamsters poured the glassful, carried it over, and drank it himself for a joke. Denker then refused to pay.

"I will absorb the cost, and gladly," said the proprietor, "if you will get out of my place. Go on, get out! Shake the dust under you, squawman. I want no more of your patronage."

Denker turned his back on him. He kept betting. He lost, lost again, and kept doubling his wager in an attempt to recoup. He was dealt two cards face down. After some hesitation, Freeze having a ten in sight, he gave the sign *hit me*. Freeze dealt him a jack. Denker fumbled with the cards and dropped one on the floor. Cards from old decks were trampled everywhere, and he picked up one of these. It was a seven of diamonds.

"That's not your card," said Freeze.

"Well, it's a seven, isn't it?"

It was obviously not the card he had dropped because it came from an old deck. Denker, however, insisted that he had dropped a seven, and if this was not his it was because his seven had fallen through a crack in the floor. Freeze, controlling his temper, turned the deck face up, stabbed out the four sevens, sorted the other cards, and said, "You're holding a four and a jack. You dropped a nine. I'll take that bet."

But Denker had pocketed it.

"It's my money, I'll take that bet," said Freeze.

"No, the bet's off. That was a fouled deck. I'll leave it to any man in the place if that wasn't a fouled deck."

Freeze got up from his stool. His hands were out of sight. Seeing him, Denker went on, but in a more whining voice:

"I only ask what's fair and square. How about it, George?" he said, addressing one of the teamsters. "I'll leave it to you if that wasn't a fouled deck."

George wouldn't answer, and moved away wanting no part of the argument.

Freeze came around the table with a pistol in his hand. He was not pointing the gun, merely holding it by the midsection, against his leg, with its muzzle toward the floor—but he had it.

"I'm telling you for the last time, give me that money."

Denker backed away. He was still unwilling to give up the bet which amounted to four dollars. He glanced toward the door evidently wondering whether he dared turn his back and walk outside. He kept backing off while Freeze strode toward him, and rammed his hindquarters into a table. The table tilted and he almost lost his balance. By accident or design he reeled toward Freeze. He had the gambler outweighed, and might easily have handled him in an eye-gouging grapple, but Freeze was ready. He had a sap concealed in his other hand. It was a tiny buckskin bag containing several ounces of shot, fastened to a thong which was looped around one of his fingers. He swung it in a sudden arc, and it would have put the big man down like an ox under the butcher's hammer, but his hatbrim deflected some of the weight, and it only staggered him.

Denker fell against a chair. His hand went to the double pistol, and he jerked it out of his sash. Freeze needed only to lift his own gun, a Navy six, but as everyone else dove for cover, Major Garside took a step and delivered a kick to his elbow. The gun flew from his hand, he turned to lunge for it, and Denker caught him with a charge of buckshot. Freeze fell on one side, a leg

53

doubled under him and his elbow propped. He rested in that position, bullet-shocked, and the second charge hit him, tearing his coat and vest and slivers from the floor.

He still seemed to be looking for the Navy. Garside kicked it across the floor and Denker clapped a foot on it. Then without taking his eyes off Freeze, he got out two paper-wrapped charges and reloaded the pistol.

The room smelled of powder, and of burning wool. Everyone commenced talking. People were on the run from other establishments. The room became crowded. A teamster took charge, had the wounded man's coat and shirt removed. They carried him to some sleeping quarters in a rear room.

"That son-of-a-bitch, he wanted to cheat me," said Denker, watching the door. "Did you see what he did? Broke the deck so nobody could find the extra card. He figured he'd have me cold with the Navy, but you got your toe in. I want to thank you. I might have got *killed* but for you!"

He spoke as if it would have been a loss irreparable to the territory.

Garside sat at an unused card table near the wall and bought a drink for Denker. The crowd was pushing around a rear door trying to see, while inside a man was pleading, "Get back, please get back. For God's sake, at least stop smoking."

Finally they fell back and gathered at the bar. They kept glancing over at Denker but made no move to approach him.

"Aren't you afraid they'll arrest you?" asked Garside.

"*Who* arrest me? They had a marshal here and he left for the gold fields. The only law here is at the fort and they don't give a hoot. Anyhow, it was self-defense,

54

pure and simple. I got right on my side. And that's sufficient in any man's town." After another whisky he said, "Naturally, there's always somebody talks hanging, especially if the accused party ain't around. However, when he is around, and armed and ready to take his own part, then they ain't quite so talkative."

Finally a man in a white apron came from the back room, most of the crowd following. There were large smears of blood on the apron. It made him look like a butcher.

Denker said, "That's Doc McDonald from down at the Drover's. He's not a real doctor. Just a lead miner. I'd rather die with the slugs in me than let him probe."

After a drink, McDonald came over and said to Denker, "Aren't you going to ask if he's still alive?"

"I don't give a damn if he's still alive."

"How is he?" asked Garside.

"He's conscious. He wants to get up." Evidently McDonald wanted to frighten Denker, but he didn't succeed.

"Tell him to," said Denker, "and that I'm loaded and waiting."

"Are you from over at the fort?" he asked Garside.

"No, I have that big wagon train north of town."

"Well, somebody said you'd been driven over in the Colonel's private wagon. I figured you might get 'em to send over their surgeon. They won't lift a finger for *us*."

"If he feels well enough to get up . . ."

"That was just talk. He's near dead. He'll die like snapping your finger if he bleeds another drop, but a surgeon, if he made it quick, might get in there and do something."

Garside got to his feet. "I have no authority, but I can mention it." He looked at Denker, "Coming?"

"No, I . . ."

"Come along!"

There was a blade of command in his voice which brought Denker heavily to his feet, and he followed outside.

"There's some business I'd like to discuss with you," said Garside. "Where can we go?"

"My shack is over here about an eighth of a mile. Is it about my townsite and the Haymeadow Butte?"

"Yes."

"That's right, you do have a party of pilgrims and no place to go. Say, this is likely to be a big night for both of us!"

It was quite dark, and there was no light in the shack. The area was a litter of broken junk which had evidently been tossed out by emigrants on the trail. There were dogs and children around. As they got close, Garside could smell rotting meat. An Indian woman had been watching their approach, but when they reached the house she was nowhere to be seen.

"That was Annie, my squaw," said Denker. "She saw you and cleared out. You want a good wife, get yourself an Injun. They know their place. You want a cup of tea? This is my daughter, Pet. Pet, Major Garside."

Pet was about seventeen, a half-breed who with her dark complexion might have been a full blood, but she was too pretty, with good nostrils and forehead, and nice lips. He could not help wondering how Denker had fathered her. She lit a lamp which consisted of a tin can, a rope wick, and what seemed to be bacon fat. The salt in the bacon kept making the flame sparkle with miniature explosions. She brought them some brassy, strong, green tea that had been steeping on the grounds.

Denker said, "Now, this is what I call *tea*. It ain't

none of that colored water they serve at the rest-au-rawnt." He got out several battered legal-brief boxes from which he took stock books, folded maps and plats, a small ledger, pens, ink, a screw-operated corporate seal, a box of gold leaf, and a book entitled *Everyman's Manual of Penmanship.*

"The Grand Central Right-of-Way Corporation!" he said, proudly holding up a stock certificate. "Ours is the cut-across and easy route to the gold fields. We're shorter than the Bozeman road by more than ninety miles, and the Bridger by more than thirty. Yet ours is the one and only road protected from hostile Indians, with fresh water at every camping spot, and belly-deep in hay."

"This is a good-looking share of stock."

"Well, it ought to be. That was printed down in Denver. The paper alone cost twelve dollars. All our corporate legal work was done by Thomas J. Dearly. I got acquainted with him in South Pass City. One of the best lawyers ever to come out of Kansas. He served on the legislature there. Union side."

"Who's this S. V. Cholin?"

He squinted it around to the light and said, "S. V. Cholin, Secretary-Treasurer." What it actually said was "S. V. Cholin, Transfer Agent." It was apparent that Denker could not read and write. "He was a real important fellow. Smart as a whip. Used to be head clerk for the Overland Freight. Then they got in on something real big and moved to Californy. Otherwise I'd never have been able to have bought control of this on my capital."

"You're the sole owner?"

"I got a few small investors around town, nothing important."

By candlelight Major Garside bent over and closely

57

examined the maps. The road had been plotted in considerable detail. The streams, springs, and camping spots were each marked and named, the distances scaled to the closest quarter-mile. A town by the name of Garden City was shown about twelve miles from Big Horn River. *See Map III,* read a notation.

"This is it," said Denker, and unfolded it for him.

Map III was drawn to a scale of an inch to the mile and covered an area from the Big Horn to the "Deepgrass Hills." He had seen no such range on another map—not even those of the Army geologists which were hung in the office at the fort—nor any kind of a town. Garden City was shown covering about a section of land. Its warehouse district was shaded in blue, its business area in pink, the residences in green. There was a projected railroad, a depot, and stock-loading yards. A courthouse was platted. Dearly County.

"We might just name that *Garside* County," said Denker, but the Major made no sign of hearing him.

Smaller towns were also mapped, many on projected road intersections. Such village names as Hannibal, Bloomington, and Elwood Corners would remind an emigrant of home. It was a nice touch, no doubt originating with lawyer Dearly. An indication of careful surveying was implicit in the name "Eighteen Mile Valley," of natural resources in "Coal Mine Road" and the "Sawlog Preserve," and of agricultural abundance in "Corn Valley" and "Orchard Bridge"; also indicated were locations of a grindstone works, a gristmill, and a communal cider press.

"I see nothing of Sage Creek."

"That name was changed to Salmon Trout Creek. We figured folks would be all fed up with sagebrush when

58

they got this far. How come you knew about Sage Creek? You familiar with that country?"

Garside had that afternoon talked with a young lieutenant who had pursued a party of raiding Gros Ventres beyond Sage Creek to the Montana boundary the summer before. The lieutenant had made no mention of any settlement, but the land itself he described as an abundant grassland, with streams running deep, cool, and swift down from the Big Horns.

"No, I've never been there." He gave Denker a shrewd look. "Have you?"

"I hope to tell you I have! I know it like the back of my hand, and I got a boy that does, too."

"Can you guide my train to Garden City and guarantee game and fuel for a winter camp?" He stopped him from too quick an answer. "I advise you not to promise something you can't fulfill."

"By God I can, and I can fulfill to the letter!" He said craftily, "Have you got some sort of a proposition?"

"I'm buying a half-interest."

"Oh, you are? For how much?"

He laid out a dollar.

"What's that?"

"I'm buying in for a dollar."

"You must be crazy."

"I'm not crazy at all. You have nothing—no town and no road. I'll furnish the town. When I get over it you'll have a road. I can make arrangements for a temporary Army post on the North Fork, permanent fort later on. Senator Carlos Trumpp will be our legal advisor in Washington. I can get an Army survey run south to Fort Steele on the Union Pacific. I'm furnishing more than you are, Denker."

Denker, in a whining voice, talked about his time and

59

expense. He made tentative mention of a thousand dollars, then of five hundred, and finally two hundred.

"I got to have at least two hundred to clean up my debts."

"If you need two hundred dollars for expenses, all you need do is say so," said Garside, Using a bullet which made a bluish metallic mark on paper, he wrote a brief statement of sale, and an even briefer expense voucher for $200. "Sign here."

With extreme labor, the squawman managed to scrawl *C. Denker* on the two papers, performing it while never quite taking his eyes off the gold pieces which were being counted from a leather bag.

With the money in his pocket, Denker got a jug of whisky and poured a good measure in two teacups. Afterward he called his family and poured some for them, too—a half-cupful for his grown son, Ignatius, and smaller quantities for Pet, fourteen-year-old John, twelve-year-old Pete, and for the younger ones, Anna, Paul, Leo, Gregory, Maria and little Luke.

"This here's Major Garside, Papa's new partner on The Road," he announced. But the crafty droop to his eyes showed he had another great piece of news. "You know that gambler that was supposed to 'uv shot all the men down in Coloraydo that folks been telling about? Well, I'll give you just one guess who it was killed him tonight."

"Was it you, Pa?" the smaller ones chorused.

"Yep, it was your own Pa! What do you think of that?"

"Did you outdraw him?" they asked, with dark eyes shining in the candlelight.

"Why, this bucko he tried to run a whizzer on me. 'Freeze,' I told him, 'you got a fouled deck.' I'll leave it

60

to the Major if he didn't try to come around for me with a Navy in his hand. He had it sort of hid against his leg. Oh, he was being *clever*. So he *thought*. But your Pa had seen that trick before. I sort of backed up careless, but all the while I had him nailed to the wall. *Pow*! I gave it to him with barrel number one. *Pow*! He got it with number two. You should have seen him hit the floor. The way his eyes were popping out! And there was two holes in him you could stick your fists into. Yes, sir, that's how your Pa served up the big, bad gunman from Coloraydo."

Later, outside, he said to Garside, "These kids of mine, being breeds, there's lots of people look down on them. I like to give 'em something to be proud of. Hold their heads up higher than other kids. It's a damn cinch none of *their* papas went out and killed themselves a gunfighter tonight."

The girl stood in the shadows and Garside could feel her dark gaze on him. He found her singularly attractive.

"You say your boy can scout for us?"

"Ignatious? You bet! And he's a good hunter to boot."

"It might be a good idea to bring your own pack outfit, set up your own camp, maintain an owner's distance— from the wagoners. Can your daughter cook?"

"That she can!"

"Think about bringing her along, also."

The stars were coming out when Garside, at a brisk walk, reappeared on the town's single street. There was still a crowd at the saloon, and men standing in front on the pole-sidewalk. The night air, which possessed a marvelous, ringing stillness at that altitude, carried their voices as if along taut wire, and he could hear the things being said. Then they saw him, and the voices quieted. They were watching to see what he would do, and he became aware of a team and wagon following him.

He turned and waited. It was the trooper with the converted ambulance.

"Oh, there you are," said Garside.

"Yes, sir. I sort of went up the road looking for you." After a while he said, "I was wondering if we ought to hurry over and get the surgeon?"

"Oh, for the gambler? Wasn't that saloon off-limits to you?"

"I didn't go inside. They came looking for me. They asked if I'd go for the surgeon. I didn't know what to do. I was supposed to wait for you, sir."

"You did the right thing."

Garside got up beside him and nodded that he was to drive on to the fort. They traveled across flatland and through the cottonwood groves for two miles without a word being spoken. The gate was open and a sentry saluted. The sounds of a melodion came from Colonel McNeel's four-room house where two women were singing a duet. They finished, and there was some applause. Garside got down, and apparently had forgotten about the surgeon. McMahon spoke.

"What about the surgeon, sir?"

"I'll speak with Colonel McNeel."

"Thanks. I wouldn't want them to think . . ."

"Want who to think? Those fellows at the saloon? I can't imagine, soldier, it being part of your duties to consider what they think."

He rapped and a Negro orderly, wearing a white jacket, let him inside.

"Colonel McNeel!" he cried. "And Mrs. McNeel, you are beautiful tonight."

The young surgeon was there, but Garside saw no reason why he should disturb his pleasant evening.

At one time the country had been the bottom of a shallow sea, and over millions of years it had accumulated thick layers of sand, silt and calcareous muds. Later, during the earth revolution which formed the Rocky Mountains, the sea bottom was lifted in a mighty bulge, and its sands and silts, pressed to solid rock, were cast in folds eastward. Later, when a rapid erosion set in, valleys were cut down through their softest parts—generally at the arch while the hard limbs of the folds remained—chopped off and angled steeply upward, forming the peculiar hogback face of northern Wyoming.

Along one of the valleys, level as a floor from hogback to hogback, and extending northward as far as the eye could see, the wagon train rolled northward. A stream—or what in some brief weeks of spring had been a stream—occupied the valley, but now it was revealed as an endlessly meandering line of buckbrush and stunted bullberries. On the level ground, sage grew to phenomenal height and scraped the undersides of the wagons, and the dust of sage rose in a choking fragrance.

The train had an Army escort as far as the North Fork. At that point—as an obvious warning to the Snakes whose young braves were showing signs of restlessness in reaction to the full-scale war that the Cheyennes and Sioux were waging in the north and east—the escort stopped in temporary fortified quarters to guard the "Haymeadow Route" on its southern flank. Thence for a number of days the traveling had been rough and slow, but lately it had leveled out—the grass was more plentiful, and the water, although scanty, was sufficient.

Garside was thus far satisfied with their progress. They were only half the distance he hoped for, but by mental surveying he saw no single serious impediment that would face a road-builder, winter or summer, or a railroad. The few slab-rock passages and declivities which had proved difficult to the wagons would quickly and cheaply yield to a blasting crew and bridge-builders. The north-south ridges which barred them from the Big Horn River in the west would soon be cut by a number of watergap passages—he had Denker's word for it, plus the evidence of the Army maps in Fort Crook. The Gileadeans would have a hard time building winter quarters when they arrived at the site, but it was one of the hardships which pioneers knew they had to endure. Sacrifice for a religious people was a thing to be sought after. Penance was an integral part of faith.

Garside slowly rode ahead of the train and up the eastern hogback. The half-breed girl, Pet Denker, was watching him. She watched him always, but thus far he had scarcely given a sign of knowing her existence. After an hour, having reached a point among the steeply-tilted rims two or three hundred feet above the valley, he stopped and rested. His eyes, narrowed and good at distance, regarded the vast panorama of country ending in some blue mountains. The wagon train was strung out in ant shapes, barely creeping. The dust hung without movement. Everything was sharply distinct, frozen by distance, in air clear as diamond.

He shucked the foil from a cigar—one of the last of the Havanas given him by Colonel McNeel as a parting gift—and while smoking he noticed that a man was watching him from a notch in the rocks about a quarter-mile away. It was Denker, who rode the remaining distance to him after realizing he'd been seen.

"You're late," said Garside. "I looked for you this morning."

"Wait'll you see what I found." With apparent relish he took a red kerchief from his belt, unrolled it, and showed three human ears. "Them's white people's ears. You'll notice they're each of different size. Also, you can see where this little white one has been pierced for a ring. That'll tell you it's a white woman's ear. She was bad mangled by wolves, and by fire, too, but it'd be my estimate she wasn't more'n twenty-five. I'd guess she was killed by accident. What I mean is, no war party will kill any twenty-five-year-old woman on purpose. They'd take turns with her, you get what I mean?"

"What was it? A wagon party?"

"Yep."

"What in hell were they doing *here*?"

"Well, we're here, aren't we? Wagons are likely to be anywhere with the gold stampede on. I counted the remains of ten wagons. Everything burned, smashed, heaped up in a coulee. Nine corpses. Scalped. Maimed. A man has to have a pretty strong gut to stand and look at a pitiful thing like that."

"Cheyennes?"

"Well, how in hell would I know? They could be Cheyennes."

"How many?"

"Couldn't tell that either. There were tracks everywhere. But it had to be twenty or more to beat that many wagons. I followed 'em a ways. There must have been tracks of fifty horses, but a lot of 'em could have been captured from the train."

"Which way did they go?"

"Nor . . . northwest."

"Toward the Big Horn?"

"A man never knows. They might be swinging around. You can't read tracks and tell what an Injun's doing."

"Where's Ignatious?"

"Scouting."

He rather suspected Ignatious, who seemed far more Indian than white, and Denker, guessing his thoughts, said, "Don't you worry about my boy. He knows Injuns like he's one of 'em. He'll camp on their trail for days and never lose sight or let 'em catch sight of him. But by God when the time comes he'll know." He offered Garside the kerchief with the ears in it. "You want these?"

"What would I want with them?"

"Well, just to show the Gileadeans, maybe. Let 'em know what a good outfit we got to take everybody through safe and sound."

"No, I'm not saying a word about this and neither are you."

"All right. You don't need to get cussed."

They parted, Denker heading toward the train, and Garside riding on to the north. A wind came up, north with the chill of snowfields. After dark he saw the sparkle of campfires at the site which Halleck had picked, and he sat for another hour, watching and listening. There was no sound except for the wolves and coyotes, and at last, chilled through, he rode back cautiously, so as not to be shot by a sentry, to where the wagons stood in the moonlight.

"Who's there?" a man challenged him. It was one of his own men, Jim Elwell.

"Garside."

"Oh. You gave me a fright."

"Everything peaceful?"

"Like the grave."

There was a lantern at one of the Gileadean wagons. The wagon was on blocks, wheels removed and soaking in a mudhole—a procedure that had become increasingly necessary in the autumn dryness. He left his horse for unsaddling and walked to his wagon. Abel Tunis was sitting asleep. Faithful black Abel, waiting to serve him his supper. He went on quietly, past the lanternlight, to the Hulbush wagon.

It gave him a start when he realized that someone was seated on some let-down steps, watching him. It was Bethel.

"You!" he said, and laughed, steadying himself. He realized that he had drawn his revolver. In the moonlight and wagon shadow he wondered if she noticed. He slid the gun away. "You scared me."

"I didn't know anything ever scared you, Brother Garside."

"Perhaps I'm afraid of you."

"What a thing to say!"

"Yes, truly."

"Why?"

"Because you're so good, so beautiful."

She sat in her nightgown, barefooted, with a shawl of crocheted blanket-strips over her shoulders. Her hair was parted and drawn back and braided thickly. She had a great deal of hair, and the braids were as thick as her wrists. Her hair had a clean fragrance—of soap, sun, and wind—and he could remember seeing her seated on these very steps, her hair combed out, drying. He wanted her hair unbraided again, cascading in brown masses; he imagined her lying across him, her hair over

67

his face. For just a second it was so strong he could almost feel the soft weight of her, and he trembled.

"Where have you been?" she asked.

He felt a surge of hope that she had been watching him . . . She had missed him.

"Away." He indicated the hills. "Out alone. I am really a very lonely man."

"Have you no family?"

"I married when I was young. Only a boy, actually. The poor girl . . . poor girl. She died after only . . . a very short time. A spirea grows on her grave. Then came the war. I wanted to die in the war. But I did not die. It put its stamp on me. The cruel war. It turned many men to stone. Is that what you meant when you said you couldn't imagine me being afraid? That I was really cold, a man of stone?"

"Oh, no, please. I'm sorry."

"Let me take hold of your hand. It means so much sometimes, only to feel the touch of a person's hands. Only the touch of someone who cares just a little. If I thought that you . . . if you cared, only a *little*, then all the cruelty and emptiness . . ." He seemed overcome. He moved and with sudden intensity said, "Bethel! Don't you understand how I need you?"

She stood up. She did not take away her hand, but she seemed to be frightened. He thought she was going to retreat inside the wagon and he wanted to stay her. He could sense her body moving freely inside the nightgown.

"Bethel. Don't misunderstand. It's as a wife."

"You are not of my people."

"I can be of them."

For a moment he thought she was going to sway into his arms. Instead she withdrew her hand and moved a

68

step higher away from him.

"I shouldn't be out here."

"Wait!" If she had gone back inside he would have followed her. Then there were footsteps and a man said, "Bethel? Daughter, is that you?"

"Papa?"

"Who's here? What are you doing up? Oh, it's you, Brother Garside."

Garside wanted him dead. "Ah, Brother Hulbush! I was just coming in from the ridge. Your daughter is a good sentry."

He talked to Hulbush for a while and said good night. At his wagon he roused Abel, had him prepare supper, ate only a few mouthfuls, and tried to sleep. He lay thinking of Bethel, and his desire for her made him get up and dress, but he did not go to the Gileadean camp; he walked down through the brush to Denker's.

"Ho, there!" he said, and after a while Denker got up, carrying his boots.

"What's the trouble?"

He knew where Pet slept and did not look that way, yet he had the sure impression she was awake, quietly watching him.

"There's something bothering the mules."

"Oh, hell. A damn mule has hearing like a fox. It's probably just echoes. These are Indiana-bred and don't understand echoes."

"There's something up the valley. I sat there for two hours after the stars were out, and something's wrong."

"What do you expect me to do?"

"God damn it, I'm not going to have the mules raided. You're the scout, go up there along the rocks. Stay for the night. I've put in my shift, you put in yours."

Cursing, Denker left, and after a few minutes Garside

saw him riding bareback out through the sage. He then looked for Pet's bed, but only the dark, unbroken bushes lay around him.

"Pet?" he said.

She did not answer, but he heard a stirring of bedrobes and sensed that she was sitting up, looking in his direction through the dark. He parted the branches and crept toward the sound, or where the sound had been— now all a blank silence.

"Pet!" he said, and the need for her was in his voice. He was aware of her nearness, her warmth, and the woodsmoke odor of her clothes and her body. Desperately hurried, he took off his boots and outer garments to get in the robes beside her. She was sitting and he was afraid she might jump up and flee from him. He reached and pulled her down across him.

"Pet! If I care for you? If I love you? If I tell you I have loved you ever since that first time I saw you!"

She did not try to get away. She remained with her weight against him.

"You love me, Pet. You've watched me every day we've been on the trail. And I love you, Pet. Would you like to be my wife?"

"Yes!" she whispered.

"Then let me make you my wife. Tonight I will make you my wife."

"There is no priest!" she whispered lying over him and her breath was warm against his ear. Every second she was more and more his, but he sensed that he must make no sharp move; it was like winning and managing a wild thing off the prairie.

"But there is no priest in a month of travel. We can't go before the Gileadeans, Pet. They aren't of your faith or mine. But when we get to a priest he will bless our union."

"He will do that?"

He knew then that it was all right, it was only a question of seconds.

"Yes, Pet! He will."

"Promise? I am your wife? Only one?"

"Yes! Promise. I promise. Yes, Pet, yes."

She was sleeping in her dress, the dress she wore always—a buckskin dress greasy from the cookfire. She moved from side to side letting him slide the dress up, her body smooth and strong beneath it.

"There is someone coming!" she whispered.

She tried to fight her way from the bed but he held her.

"Don't move!" he whispered savagely. "Be quiet."

Someone had walked to the glowing remnants of the cookfire. It was one of the hunters standing as sentry come to look for a heel of tea in the pot. They lay without breathing, while he shook the pot and turned away. Garside, silent but firm, returned to his need, and suddenly she forgot the sentry who was leaving—forgot everything except the man, her man—and she gave herself utterly. I will treat her well, Garside thought afterward. I will not forget her. I will come to her again and again. He remained and rested with her body between him and the ground. I will have to take a bath to remove the smoky odor, he thought. It's strange how squaws keep that smoky odor even out in the sun and wind. He wondered if she was lousy, but it was too late to worry now. It was not her fault that she was a breed. And he let her run her fingers through his hair, and to whisper in his ear, "My husband, my darling husband."

✧✧✧

71

Garside awoke next morning feeling more secure and content than he had for weeks. The arrangement with Pet was as ideal as he could wish for. He was a man with frequent need for a woman, and things had been difficult for him since he had left Mrs. Griswold behind at LaBonte. Because she was a breed, Pet would not be demanding. Indians and half-Indians were used to such moonlight arrangements. If he got her with child, it would be quite all right. It would not show before they reached Garden City, and he could send her on to Montana. People would not particularly suspect him, for it was assumed that breed girls slept with everybody. He might find her a husband. His own cousin-by-law, redhead Dave Halleck, immediately came to mind. Dave was always watching Pet from a distance, or calling when she was busy around the camp. He might even, finally, see to it that Dave and Pet got in the robes together, and in this way cause Dave to believe that the offspring was his. The situation offered numerous solutions.

His contemplation was interrupted by the appearance of Indian riders along the western ridge. There were nineteen of them by count. After half a day of appearing and reappearing along the rims, a representation of four came down and asked for gifts. They were Snakes, they indicated by sign language, out to raid the Cheyennes, and had only warmest feelings for the Cheyenne's enemies, the white men. What they wished in payment for the train traversing their country were rifles and metallic ammunition, flour, tobacco, and a jug of strongwater. Garside gave them each a quarter-pound of tobacco and sent them away. Their companions had stopped on the hill just out of rifle-range and when the four had covered about half that distance one of them turned, lifted his old long-barreled cap-and-ball rifle and shot a Gileadean mule, dropping it like a stone in the traces.

The action was so unexpected that the Indians escaped without a shot being fired at them. The train stopped while the dead mule was being rolled from the harness and a broken hame repaired. One of the hunters, a man named Cox, who had made one trip to Oregon on the trail, advised that the mule be butchered-out because game was growing very scarce, what with Indians combing the country; but the Gileadeans were repelled at the idea, and the Methodists were unwilling to take their leavings.

"Finding game is your job," Halleck said to him.

"It may be my job, but it'll be a dead man's job if I stir more than a mile from this train."

The Indians followed them day after day, and in the early morning there were signal smokes. At times as many as seventy of them were in full view, riding miles apart on opposite ridges signaling with mirrors and with fires and with blankets. Then suddenly all of them disappeared and Ignatious Denker rode in with a tale of having been severed from the train by at least three war parties moving between there and the Big Horn. And he reported not only Snakes, but Arapahoes and Blackfeet.

"That's ridiculous," said Garside who thought the boy was merely building his importance as a scout. "The Blackfeet are north of the Three Forks."

But Ignatious, with his Indian truculence, let the words wash off from him. He had the annoying way of never seeming to hear a word he did not want to, and never arguing when contradicted.

"The boy knows Indians," said Denker.

"I don't want any of this to reach the Gileadeans.

They're upset enough already, and Reverend Klinkke would like to lead them all to Montana so he can missionary at the gold camps. How many do you estimate—total?"

Ignatious merely looked at him.

"How many?"

"Answer him," said Denker.

"Two thousand."

Garside laughed. It named him a liar. It was like spit in his face.

"How many?"

He did not seem to hear him.

"How many!"

"He said two thousand," said Denker.

"Let him say it."

"He already said it."

"And I say it's a lie. He wants to be a hero."

"He didn't claim to have counted 'em. He was making a guess."

"I don't want guesses. I want to know."

Garside was not afraid of Indians, and gave no credence to the fantastic estimate of two thousand, but he feared the resolve of his wagoners—the ridge passage which was to lead them to Garden City was unpredictably far to the north. For three successive days there was not a sign of Indians, then one quiet afternoon (when it was so serene that a person could ride clear of the wagons and hear the autumn crickets) twenty savages rose apparently from nowhere and rode whooping down on a wayward wagon—one of the outfits picked up at LaBonte—and killed the owner and his mulatto helper. In the four or five minutes required to organize a counter-attack, their bodies had been stripped, scalped, baggage torn apart and robbed, and

74

then the Indians rode away, driving the team with the harness still on them, one daredevil brave standing on his horse inviting a bullet.

Scouting became more difficult and hunting almost impossible. The wagon train was tightened, and by Garside's order broken outfits were left behind. The traditional wagon-train circle was obviously impossible in most of the terrain, so he trained them in a forward-wagons-outward and rear-wagons-inward telescope maneuver to form a square.

There were no further attacks, but alarms were of almost hourly occurrence as parties of riders delighted in feints and passes, high-speed charges that were pulled to just at the edge of rifle-range, and nightly attempts to run off the grazing horses.

The plan had been to cross over at a place called the Pollit Saddle. This windgap of the western ridge was marked on all the Army maps, and Denker claimed to have scouted it on one of his long north travels weeks before, but the days passed with nothing like a windgap showing itself and Denker maintained they had passed it during some hours of low clouds and storm. The maps, however, showed other passes to the north. In a predicted three days they would be at the Portuguese Flats where all the hogbacks north and south terminated in a flatground of sand and dried lakes. There were said to be large groves of cottonwoods at the Flats, it was a famed hunting country where the deer and wapiti came down from the high country of the Big Horns during storm, and where antelope and buffalo might be found in any season. Garside called a meeting of the Gileadeans to describe the area and point out that, while they were indeed ten to twenty days off their intended schedule, the flats would offer an admirable opportunity to lay in supplies of meat—either dried or chilled depending on the weather—and a few days' sojourn in the deep grass would put needed strength in the livestock.

It was cold and windy that night, and dawn came through a bullet-colored sky. In the afternoon it started to rain. It rained steadily, and it was cold. The stream began to run. It rose so every crossing was at least hub-deep in mud. The wagons mired and some were unhitched so extra teams could move the others, then the teams had to come back, and they struggled on.

The rain lasted for two days, and was followed by a pale, autumn sunlight. The mountains lay white under snow, and there were snow edgings along the east and west ridges. Indians still rode along the rocks. Then the valley broadened and the Portuguese Flats lay ahead of them—a great stretch of marsh and little, drying sand dunes.

At last they were on a well-defined road, but it led to the east rather than the west, and after some miles played out in a morass of sand and tiny ponds. A new route was hunted along some benches which at last led to the promised meadows and cottonwood groves, but if there was a pass, a thousand acres of muck barred the way.

They camped to rest the beaten-out stock, and the Gileadeans set to work gathering the waist-deep grass and roping it in great bundles on their wagons. In this they were fortunate to have the transport and the labor. Most of the emigrants were loaded to the capacity of their creaking outfits and did not have the women and children as reapers.

There was another meeting and many of the emigrants were for returning south to find the Pollit

Saddle. Others scoffed that such a pass existed. The opinion became current that they had somehow come up from the Tensleep Country one valley too far to the east, on the wrong side of the Portuguese Flats, hopelessly misplaced in regard to the Big Horn; hence there was left only one escape in the weeks remaining—to travel northward and somehow make a passage to Montana between the mountains and the canyon.

It stormed again. They were a week getting around an eastward protuberance of the flats. The rain turned to snow. In the morning there was frost in the ground to carry them, so they traveled in the hours between midnight and sunup, until at last the sand and the ponds were behind. They traveled up a valley once more, but narrower, in places almost a canyon between the rock-faced hogbacks. Horses died and the Gileadeans refused to share any of their precious hay. A Gileadean, Joseph Pennywell, was found dead with a large caliber bullet through him, and there were mutterings against a wagoner named Jim Cowan with whom he had quarreled.

The days were becoming short. Sometimes it seemed that the train barely got hitched and started when darkness came. Then a freezing wind blew in from the north carrying little, hissing pellets of snow, and the snow increased to become a blizzard.

There were complaints that the train should camp and wait out the storm, but Garside would not hear them and he ordered it to go on. It moved at a mile-in-two-hours crawl, and when he could stand it no longer, he had his horse Abelard saddled and rode out along the ridge looking for some place where a switchback could be dug; but beyond that ridge there were more ridges and more. He came back wet through and his clothes frozen in lumps. He went to bed in his wagon too tired to eat more than a bite of the supper his faithful Abel Tunis had prepared for him. He slept and a sound awakened him.

"What was that?" he asked. Abel did not answer. He got up and walked barefooted to the door. Abel was a dark figure against the snow, and he was watching something.

"Oh, Mist' Major. I didn't hear you. Somebody just hove into camp."

"It's probably Ignatious."

"No sir. They're strangers. They on the run from them savages. I did hear shootin' earlier in the day."

The hunter Cox walked over with the news that one of the men was wounded.

"That's just what we have need of," said Garside. "Some wounded renegades to care for."

If Garside had met with a wounded renegade he would simply have put him out of his misery, but the fellows were there now, and nothing he could do about it.

He dressed and went over. The crowd quieted, and opened for him. Someone was holding a smoky pitch-torch inviting bullets from any make-brave Indian who crawled up through the shadows. Its light fell on a couple of saddle-horses, a big bay and a roan that looked as if it were ready to fall, and more distantly on a mule-eared packhorse. Aldo Rimmel, whom Garside disliked, was directing the loutish Fisher boy and a couple of others in unsaddling and rubbing the horses free of ice.

"Where are they?" asked Garside.

A man came forward. He was stocky and whiskered

with the appearance of having spent days and weeks in the brush.

"I'm one of 'em. I'm Bob Tiller. Some call me Doc."

"Garside."

Doc Tiller offered to shake hands but Garside took no notice.

"You a doctor?"

"No, they just call me that."

"Where's the other one?"

"McCoy?"

"I don't know what his name is. I was told there was a wounded man came in."

"Yah, well they took him someplace."

"He's over at the Gileadean wagons." said Aldo. "They were going to fix him up."

"Where were you headed?"

"We were heading down from Montana. These Indians got wind of us and we had to hit for the coulees. We been riding days and sleeping nights for a week. Then we rode into the middle of 'em and had to run for it."

"What Indians were they?"

"They were hellish Indians."

The man laughed, Garside did not even smile. "I asked you a question."

"Well, they might have been Shoshone. They seemed to be headed to winter camp from that hole-in-the-wall country south and east of the Big Horns. That would make them Shoshones, Arapahoes . . . one of those tribes. We figured maybe they were up that way on the fall hunt."

"How many were there?"

"I'd say at least a hundred, There were two bands."

"All right. I guess you'll make out. How bad is he . . . your partner?"

"He took one alongside the head."

79

"One what?"

"We were riding down this draw and it was dark. We run into a whole mess of them. I think he got hit by a lance. Sort of clubbed with it. In the head."

"Was he able to ride?"

"Oh, he hung on all right, with help."

"There's blood all down the side of the horse," somebody said.

Garside walked to the Gileadean camp and saw with an added twitch of annoyance that a light was on in the Hulbush wagon, the one Bethel slept in. He might have known—they couldn't pick up so much as a crippled coyote puppy along the trail but she would take it and care for it. He didn't mind the puppies—he rather liked her for it, and to see her gentle way with her hands—but dragging a young renegade to her wagon . . . to her very bed!

"How is he?" he asked old Hulbush, finding him shivering outside.

"He was struck down fearsomely, and there was so much blood and swelling it's hard to tell. It may be his eye is mashed out and it may be it isn't. She's sponging off it now. He's raving and fevered."

"Do you think it's a good thing to leave her there with a man raving and fevered?"

"When one gives mercy and charity it is not to consider such things, Brother Garside."

He stood and looked at the wagon. No sound came from inside.

Hulbush said, "I think if we could have only a dram of your brandy . . ."

"I'm sorry, Elder, but when Bernhard was down with lung fever we gave all but the last emergency drop of it. Why don't you see Kavanaugh? He still manages to keep a barrel of wheat wine fermenting in his wagon."

"No, this man is in need of brandy, but I wouldn't ask for the last emergency drop of it."

Garside returned to his quarters. There, reminded of the brandy, he opened a fresh quart and drank off a glassful. It was Virginia brandy, the best since before the war, and it sprang back through each separate fiber of his body with a bright strong fire.

He got up before dawn and ordered Abel to blow the bugle which was the morning signal to awake and start. It was still storming, but the secret was to go on and on. That afternoon when he stopped the wagon for a bite to eat—he never munched while riding or walking like the others, but stopped and had his table set—Dennis came around to say the wounded man was awake, and rational, and spreading fear among the Gileadeans that Garden City meant a winter of famine.

Garside took no action immediately. But that night he went to the wagon, routed him, out, got him down in the snow barefooted and had a look at the face. The man who called himself Doc Tiller showed fight, and Garside almost had the excuse of killing him, but Aldo Rimmel interfered; however the state of the renegade McCoy's face was a substitute satisfaction.

"Get the lantern higher," he said. He hunted for the correct grip to bear down and tear the split bones free. With a twist and sudden thumb pressure he felt the cheek go crack! Ramming his knee, he held the writhing man against a wagon wheel. He ground the bones back and forth. The man wilted under the torture, and he felt a sudden, marvelous release. It gave him a triumphant feeling. It was like walking from an overheated room into the bright air again. He let him fall.

"No, bandage be damned," he said. "Let him go. He'll get up all right."

They had all wanted to stop him. But none of them had. Weaklings! They would get together and plot behind his back, but when the time came not one of them had the guts to face him. They were swine and his manner was like spit on them.

"His cheek was broken. I had to set the bones in place. Now if he has any guts he'll keep up and around and cure himself. If we wrap him in bandage he'll never be able to use the jaw again."

Lips twisted in distaste, he used a clean handkerchief to wipe blood from his fingers. He tossed it to Abel not wishing to touch it again before it was laundered. The man still lay in the snow. His face would be crooked forever, and every time he looked in a mirror he would remember how it was an excellent idea to mind his own business and not spread stories to the detriment of another.

Later, tired, but with the feeling of a task well done, he left his wagon and walked a long way through the sleeping camp to the place in some juniper where he knew Pets robes were spread. She was awake and waiting for him.

She was quiet and strong and competent. She was always so and often he visited her, and was satisfied, and slept for a while and left again without more than a whispered word or two being exchanged. But tonight she was different, and after receiving him she said, "Do you know I will have your baby?"

It did not anger Garside. Rather it gave him a pleasurable sense of accomplishment. It was a complication, but rather expected. It meant he would have to move Pet away from sight of the Gileadeans, but another month or two would do. He lay in deep fulfillment in the widespread saddle of her legs—her ample abdomen between his loins and the ground—and had mellowing, comforting thoughts. Particularly if the child proved to be male he resolved not to lose track of him. He would provide for him, observe his development, and, should he prove worthy, take him into his employment. Even adopt him. A Garside!

CHAPTER 3

MCCOY HAD HIS FIRST SHAVE IN MANY DAYS, AND after getting accustomed to the new feel of nakedness in the cold he felt better. He could drive now, and see a little out of his puffy eye. The pain was steady, but it would settle to a dull beat that allowed whole hours to pass, his mind elsewhere.

The storm had passed over. Each morning you got up in the pre-dawn under stars that were bright and hard. Your boots were frozen, and you pulled them on like hollowed-out pieces of stone and trod through the hot camp ashes to thaw them for walking. You hitched the teams while everything was cold and harsh, and there was shouting and gee-hawing and cursing and the groan of frozen wagons. If there was a creek crossing it helped to get going early when the ice was thickest. Although the first wagon always broke through, the mud beneath would be stiff and the broken chunks of ice ground in for an added solidity. Later in the day when the sun shone and the air rose above freezing such crossings became a seethe of muck, slush and fresh manure— hoof-punched and rutted, slippery as beaver slides.

From a distance McCoy glimpsed Bethel driving her

father's big wagon. She was very competent with the four-mule team. And he saw Garside riding a large gray horse with his back as stiff as the steel engravings of Union generals at Spottsylvania. He wanted to put a bullet between Garside's shoulders. The feeling, for it was a real one, made him wince, for it could only mean that he was afraid of him. No matter what the front he put on, he was afraid of the Major. And yet someday he would have to face him. If not at the turn off when the Rimmel boys and the others wanted him to guide them north, then later. Eventually he would have to have it out with Garside and he was afraid of him. Why? He had been a dozen places with as good a chance of getting killed, and he had not felt any particular fear until afterward. But he was afraid of Garside.

He tried not to think about him. There was no stop for the noon meal. The days were growing short, and suddenly it was twilight. It was a clear twilight and one could see the Big Horns, massive and white, with purplish canyons and cliffs like broken battlements. The north wind blew through them and there was an odor of pines.

Chuck Rimmel cooked a supper using meat from a horse that had fallen and a few roots dug by the Fisher kids who traded them for cartridges. There was some quiet talk in progress, and Doc came around.

"You feel able to ride?"

"Of course I can ride. What is it?"

"He's about to swing out of here. Garside. There's finally a pass and he's taking it back toward his city. Kavanaugh gave Elwell a little liquor, and he told him. Primus Creek. It cuts srtaight across all these ridges. The boys want to make a break north, and us to guide them."

"I think they're being a pack of damn fools."

84

"You mean on account of the Indians?" asked Chuck.

"Yes, I mean on account of the Indians. Twenty or twenty-five men—they'll cut us to pieces."

"You got through, didn't you?"

"We didn't have wagons."

"Are you backing out?"

"I can't back out from something I didn't enlist in in the first place."

"God damn it, they're planning on us," said Doc. "We just the same as promised. If you don't want to go, all right. But I'll go without you."

"I didn't say I wouldn't go, Doc. I didn't say one way or the other."

He didn't want to ride off and turn over that sweet Hulbush girl to the Major. And because he feared the Major, it seemed like running away.

"Who else is going?"

"Tonight? Just Aldo."

"All right, I'll get my horse."

"If your face is too bad . . ."

"No, I'll go."

The horses were saddled. They rode from the camp by a side route into some box elder trees that still had a few leaves hanging on them. A sentry was there. He was one of their own bunch.

"How's it look?" asked Doc.

"Quiet as the grave."

They rode with Doc muttering, "What a hell of a thing to say. I'm not scared of dying, but I go sick every time I think of being buried here in this cold. Just lying there frozen forever. Don't you ever get a feeling like that?"

Aldo said, "You shouldn't let your mind dwell on those things. I'm headed for Montana where it's even

85

colder, but I think about making my stake silver-mining. Then I'm going back home and buy a store and have a big farm at the edge of town. I'm going to raise corn and trotting horses and smoke my own pork. I'm not going to die until I'm ninety years old, and I'll have grandchildren and everything. That's the kind of stuff I think about."

The camp was left behind. It seemed very quiet. The valley they followed was not wide, and it had patchy cover for lurking Indians, but the cold was a sort of protection. Nobody, Indian or white, stayed out on such a night just on the chance of getting a potshot. The Indians would be in a camp of their own, willows tied over, robes spread for a roof, and a few coals glowing. Or when it got really bad they might build little pit fires, cover them with sods, and curl belly-down taking in warmth through the ground.

"How far did Elwell say it was?" asked McCoy.

Aldo said, "I'm not sure. Kavanaugh talked to him. He seemed to think it was less than a day by wagon. In that case we can get the lay of the land and be back by dawn."

"Has he been there?"

"Elwell? No, it was scouted by that kid of Denker's. But it seemed to be a well-known pass. They used to drive wooden-wheel carts over it in the fur-trade days. Elwell thinks Garside will have to dig roads across the rough parts. It'll take a couple of days, but I think we better roll straight on before he knows what's doing. But that's up to you, Morg. We'll do what you say."

"What if I say not to split off at all?"

He didn't answer. The bottoms became brushy and cut by side gullies. It was slow going in the dark. It would be slow going next day for the wagons. They rode in silence.

86

Cold seemed to sharpen the senses and one heard the echoes of hoofs rather than the hoofs themselves. And the sudden light and dark of the night shadows continually startled them as from the appearance of an enemy. The sides finally fell away; they climbed a dirt bank where the stream made a wide meander, and emerged on some extensive flats. There was brush along the streams, several of which seemed to meet, and groves of aspens on the flats. The aspens looked white as the snow by moonlight, with their tops a light gray. The hogback was chopped into hills and conifers grew black in the more sheltered and steeper areas.

"We're close to the mountains here," Doc said. "You can tell that mountain feeling in the air. It smells like Montana. If we really got 'em to rolling there's not a wagon aside from the Holy Joes that wouldn't quit him and go north. And I'm not so sure about the Holy Joes."

"I am," said McCoy, "and they aren't quitting him."

"How about Reverend Klinkke?"

"I don't know about him, but Hulbush isn't. And they'll follow Hulbush. Probably even Klinkke will follow him."

The old cart road was distinguishable as a winding line through the bushes and a white smoothness of snow where it slanted up the deep draw to the west. Enlarged by darkness the draw seemed to enter a mountain range, forbidding and endless.

They rode past, and out on the flats. There was a faint smell of horses, and the snow became dappled by hoofs. Aldo got down to look.

"There must be hundreds of 'em."

"Did Ignatius mention this?"

"I don't know. It's a cinch Elwell didn't, or Kavanaugh would have told me."

"You still want to head for Montana?"

"Yes, I still want to head for Montana. At least we'll be fighting to get someplace and not just a dying spot off on the freeze-out. Anyhow, these tracks aren't new. There's snow in all of 'em. The manure's all frozen." He kicked at it. "It thawed and froze in again. It must be a couple or three days old. These fellows might be through the pass and fifty miles away by this time. They might be over in Garden City waiting for *them*."

"The thing for us to do is join the tribe," McCoy said good-humoredly. "We'd probably have meat for the winter, shelter, fuel, squaws, everything."

"This is serious business. When we get here, I'm for rolling right straight on for Montana. I don't want a fight with him, he's got us outnumbered. Nine in that private army of his—eleven counting him and Tunis— and then Denker's crowd, and all those Holy Joes if trouble really started. But it's one thing to stop us in a face-off, and another to bring us back if we're gone."

"Then its simple. The Gileadeans always want to roll first and have first chance at the grass. We'll make a second line and come around over there to the east. The Gileadeans will grab the meadow and we'll go right past and nobody will think much of it. It'll look like we're heading for some other wood and pasture. Only we won't stop. We'll keep on going. We'd better ride up yonder a mile or so and have a look at what we have to cross. If there's a draw or a creek we'd better pick out crossing now."

Doc said to Aldo, "Do you think Garside will try to stop us?"

"No, I don't. Not if it looks like shooting. He can't afford to lose any men."

But he said it without too much conviction.

It was almost morning and they could hear the crowing of roosters in the Gileadean camp when they returned. Deadly tired, McCoy went inside the wagon and fell on his face across the blanket-rolls.

"Hey, don't you want some breakfast?" asked Chuck Rimmel through the end-gate door.

"Not now. I have to rest."

He woke up when the wagon stopped. It was nine o'clock by the flip-open watch inscribed *To Morgan McCoy an his Twenty-first Birthday*. Aldo Rimmel was driving. He got up and stood behind him looking at the wagons which were jammed in together between a cutbank and the creek. On slightly higher ground, along a bench, horsemen rode single-file with their rifles out.

"Is there trouble?"

"I don't know. I haven't seen a thing. Garside called all troopers out, then he beefed up with about eight from our wagons—all we could spare. Why in hell don't he draft some of these Gileadeans when the danger shows?"

"Anyhow, this is our last day."

"Uh-huh," he said, not too sure about it.

"Haven't you had any sleep?"

"I slept for a while. You better go get some breakfast. Mrs. Kavanaugh might have a cold dough-god."

The train got to rolling again. It went a few wagons at a time—start, stop, and start again. Mrs. Kavanaugh gave him a tin cup of yeasty wheat wine and marked down 25¢ in her records which she kept on the canvas. There was no food left. He helped her with the job of holding the wine barrels in place while her husband drove, coping with a steep declivity and an even steeper, twisting, climb up and over. After him came the

89

Bowers' wagon with Mrs. Bowers driving, her husband being one of those drafted for cavalry duty by Garside.

She got stalled as Kavanaugh expected and had to be given a jerkline. They moved on through the spotty thickets and cutbank turnings through which McCoy had ridden the night before. There were bullberries still hanging in scarlet clusters on the leafless bushes and the wagons slowed while people got out to pick them hurriedly before all were gone to the "hogall" Gileadeans. A deer was startled and ran amid the wagons, horns up and zig-zag, leaping while bullets whizzed around him, until Kavanaugh brought him to earth. Half-a-dozen wagoners came running to get it quartered and out of sight, but Garside rode up, stiff-backed and powerful with his feet thrust hard in the stirrups and said, "Take that carcass to the commissary wagon. It'll be divided. You'll get your share."

They obeyed him. It was noon and the sun was breaking through. Doc rode back from a forward lookout and signaled that the big flat was around the next turning. McCoy had saddled his bay horse. Quietly, the column had been forming—Aldo Rimmel, Kavanaugh, Mrs. Bowers, the two Fisher wagons, Crane and several more. It looked as if Stewart had joined in, and Arvold and the bachelor McCrae. He rode back to see whether Aldo was ready. It would be Aldo's job to lead the column, commence its right-side swing that would break it free of the train, and head for the north.

But Aldo had stopped. Garside had his horse crosswise of the trail. His men—Lindstrom, Ellis, Dennis—were behind him and their rifles were ready. And he had Cox and Barrow on higher ground.

"What's the trouble?" Aldo asked.

"Get down."

"What for?"

"I said to get down, isn't that enough?"

While Aldo was tying the reins around the handbrake, Garside dismounted. He walked around the team and watched while Aldo lowered his big form. And without warning, Garside hit him.

Aldo went down, striking the ground so hard his hat was sent rolling for twenty feet. Both McCoy and Doc had turned their horses, and Doc had his gun half from its scabbard when Garside's men rode in. It was well-timed.

"I don't want to do it, boys!" said Dennis with his rifle across the saddle horn. "You stay back. This is between the boss and Aldo."

There was nothing to do but watch. Garside did not glance at them. He stood, breathing through his nostrils, rubbing his right fist, while Aldo sat up. He waited until Aldo grabbed for the wagon wheel and reeled to his feet. Then, stepping and timing with brutal perfection, he hit him again.

This time the big fellow was driven head and shoulder solid against the wagon wheel. He held to the spokes with one hand, without awareness. His eyes were knocked off-focus, his mouth drooped open, and hair was spilled across his forehead.

"You're at the head of these deserters, aren't you?" Garside said. "I was wondering when you'd build up guts enough to make your run. So you picked this spot here. Here, where we need you the most! Just when we need every man to run the pass. Oh, that was the smart way of doing it! Now listen! I want everybody to hear this. If brave Aldo wants to leave all he has to do is get me out of the way!"

Aldo tried to get up. He sank to his hands and knees.

91

Garside seized him by the hair, hauled him forward, stood him, balanced him on his wobbly legs, and hurled him falling against the wagon sheel. The side of his head struck steel, but he still retained a measure of consciousness. Garside stepped in and kicked him. He used the icy heel and sole of his boot and kicked him again and again.

McCoy spurred forward, trying to ride his horse between them, and received a blow from Dennis' rifle stock that knocked him to the ground. His horse bolted and the diversion broke in on Garside's preoccupation, so he stopped to look. Aldo was on knees and elbows bleeding from ear and mouth. His right ear had been torn half-off and each time Garside kicked him it had flopped, spraying blood. Garside saw that blood had been spattered across the knees of his trousers and, with distaste, picked up snow to scrub it off. He looked at McCoy without much interest. He remounted and started issuing orders:

"All right, swing to there! Nobody's breaking off for Montana. We'll camp here and have a look at the pass. Kavanaugh, lead the rear column over right oblique! Roll!" He said to McCoy, "Up, there! Get this man in his wagon. Get it rolling!" And as he rode off they could still hear him. "Brother Zuph, give to the left, we're forming two ranks. We have room to circle in the flats beyond the trees. Halt now, and you, Klinkke, gee around the big tree . . ."

"How do you feel?" Dennis said to McCoy who was on his feet, waiting for his horse to be brought back.

"How do you think I feel," he said, rubbing the back of his neck.

"Do you realize we had orders to shoot to kill? If I

hadn't hit you somebody would have done it. Linstrom would have done it. I saved your life, do you know that?"

"Yah, maybe you did. But I'll be lucky to live through all the help I'm getting."

"You're alive. And as for big Aldo, he had it coming. He was asking for it."

McCoy thought he had it coming, too. They all had it coming for trying to make a sneak run instead of walking up and having it out with Garside face to face. And there was something in what Garside said about deserting him at the moment he needed them most. What would I do in his position? McCoy wondered, and the question went unanswered.

He helped get Aldo inside the wagon. He was quite a problem. He would lie almost limp for a time, then he would rise and flail with his fists, taking three men to hold him. When they reached the flats they decided to get him outside and walk him around. Finally he was settled enough to sit while Mrs. Kavanaugh sewed his ear back on and bound it to his head with strips of flour sacking.

"This is good stuff to have on it," she said. "It's never been washed, and the flour in it will help glob the blood."

Dennis then rode down with a list of names for the special detail which was to set out under Garside's command to explore the pass. McCoy heard his name called. There were eighteen men, half of them Garside employees. Zuph Brockway was there from the Gileadean wagons—a concession to those who had been complaining that the Gileadeans were "living on the fat of the land" and never taking a chance. But Zuph kept coming around to ask McCoy about the gold camps, so perhaps Garside would willingly have him killed as a divisive influence. All were horseback except Abel Tunis who drove one of the Major's "Antietam" wagons. The wagon was lightly loaded with ammunition, a sawed-off swivel gun, a few blankets, and food for a day or so. The Major apparently had it in mind to set up an outpost somewhere midway along the deep, timbered V of the pass, and he kept studying one place and another with a small, brass telescope.

What had looked like a road was actually an old travois trail. It was wider than the gauge of the wagon, and Abel drove always with one side several inches higher than the other. The snow was a mass of horse tracks, but no travois had gone over since the storm.

They came to an old camp. There were many moccasin tracks. Bushes were tied together with twisted grass. Robes had been laid over them, but aside for one rat-eaten old buffalo hide the robes had been removed. Bones were strewn through the snow, gnawed by wolves. They were large bones, probably of buffalo. Beneath a half-burned log some coals were smoldering.

Discovery of the fire resulted in a hair-trigger nervousness, a noticeable reluctance to go on.

McCoy said, "That fire might have been creeping through the wood rot for a week or ten days. They can get real deep and burn all winter."

"Would you say this was a hunting party?" asked Bowers hopefully.

"Maybe the thing they're hunting is us."

"Where the hell's our scout?" asked Cox.

Ignatius Denker was on the ridge, and they waited for him. When half an hour passed without him appearing, Garside asked for volunteers, sending McCoy and Elwell.

From higher ground the pass did not seem so deep-cut

94

or timbered. The peaks looked like knolls when one approached them, and there was grass sticking up through the snow. The travois trail was distinguishable for five miles or so. Only its first portion was steep. For the most part its course took it along the edge of a brushy creek. Here and there it twisted through some little hills, each with a knob of rock on top. In the distance it disappeared into rolling country with timber. The draws had gathered a winter purple. In places the purple had a dense slate hue, the residue of early cookfires. Not a horse, man, or shelter was visible, but as McCoy looked he had the uneasy feeling that something had just escaped the eye, that there was movement somewhere—but hidden, elusive.

Across, far across, he saw Elwell. Elwell waved his hat in a wide sweep and he waved back. When the hat continued it was apparent he was trying to impart some information. Apparently he had lost sight of the wagon and main body of men who were in plain view to McCoy, and he wanted to relay something. Then he lifted his rifle and fired.

The shot was an emergency signal of danger. One could see the jump of power-smoke from the barrel for seconds before the crack and echoes came. Then McCoy saw other smokes jump up from a rock reef and Elwell's sudden turning. The shots came in a rattle after Elwell went down on hindquarters to the ground. He was holding to his bridle and crawling while the horse tried to escape. It became apparent he was not wounded, that he was deliberately letting the horse pull him downhill to a place behind scrub pines where he could mount in reasonable safety.

Below, Garside rode out from his column, still not able to see what was happening. He glimpsed McCoy who had turned and was picking his way as rapidly as possible downhill. *Keep going, keep going,* McCoy signaled because if an attack came the main body would be caught like fish in a barrel. Instead, Abel Tunis, standing in the wagon, drew up.

"Keep going!" he shouted.

Tunis then heard him and began whipping the rumps of his team. The wagon was light; they took it at a rattling clip uphill over little pitches, then up a very steep pitch, and out to a naked bench between the creek and the hill. Tunis stopped, and Jack Veach, a Colorado man working for Garside, coming from a forward position to signal him, was caught in a volley and dropped from his horse.

He was lying apparently dead and his horse drifting sidewise, careful not to step on the bridle reins, when McCoy had his final glimpse before descending into the trees. He picked a way over windfalls, expecting every step to stir up an ambush, but nothing happened. He rode through some shallow snow with the wagon in view. Abel was gee-hawing it, and men were placing themselves inside behind some heavy planking, and here and there along the creek at Garside's direction. He lost sight of all but the flat roof of the wagon; and when he came up it was unhitched, the team out of sight, everyone out of sight except for Garside who signaled for him to dismount. He did, a couple of men spoke to him, and he joined them along an old high-water bank of the creek. A 180-degree sweep of the up-country was visible to them there, and a group of Indians were in view riding straight down the slope. They did not seem to realize how close they were until they saw the wagon. There were seven of them; they wheeled and rode off at a gallop, other riders joined them, then they came in a two-pronged charge. They were met by a fire that took three of them off their horses—the one charge veered and the other stopped altogether, and in the stillness after gunfire they could be heard crashing through the brush and calling to one another in the peculiar, sharp accents of their language. Out of range more Indians rode down from the hill to join them.

After a while Veach came crawling in, doggedly, about six inches at a time, leaving a streak of blood behind him in the snow. When it was safe to do so, and quite a while after the men wished to do it, Garside gave the signal to go help him.

They opened Veach's shirt which was heavy with blood and saw that he had taken a bullet almost directly through the navel.

"This fellow rode out on his own," said Garside, "and you see what he got for it."

He lay on his back sucking breath, drawing his stomach hollow under his rib cage from the muscular contortion of breathing against pain, and he looked up at Garside.

"Can you probe for it?" someone asked.

"There's no use of probing for it. Probe and he bleeds to death."

"Oh, Christ!" whispered Veach. "Do something."

"You're going to die, Mister."

Veach lay and looked at him.

"Maybe we ought to pack the wound with tobacco," said Zuph.

"Go right ahead, if you can waste the tobacco."

Tunis said, "You know what's also good for a belly wound? Burying in mud. Just absolutely right up to the armpits in mud."

"Your job is with the team and not treating people

97

with mud."

"Yes, sir."

Garside re-formed his men in three groups so each would give protection to the others; some logs, hurriedly tossed up like a fortification, would later prove empty. The Indians making signal noises and continually shifting positions were setting up for an attack. When it came, only the men in the wagon were where the Indians thought they would be, and these, protected by heavy oak, aimed a cruel fire through the rifle slots.

The fight lasted in full violence for only a minute or so. The Indians were in large numbers, but for the most part poorly armed, half of them with no more than bows and arrows, and most of the rifles old-Jeagers and converted flintlocks. Then, while some charged, others retreated, and afterward there was a desultory fire in volleys and silences, and a man could be heard moaning in the brush.

"They got Moore," said Cox.

"No, he's yonder," said Tunis.

"Where?" asked Garside.

"Yonder, down the road."

Moore had retreated from the place Garside had assigned him to a place better protected about fifty yards away, and now they could see him—a bushy-haired, bucktoothed fellow of about twenty-one—continually stealing his head into view and ducking it back again, fearing a return to the main group because of some Indian sharpshooters who had nested themselves high up on the other side of the creek.

"Moore!" Fisher called to him. "Moore, can you hear me?"

"Yah!"

"Well, listen. We'll sneak over and keep them down with a steady fire. Then when we signal, you run for it."

"What?"

He started to repeat, but Garside checked him.

"Wait. Moore!"

"Yah?"

He sounded more frightened of Garside than of the Indians.

"You abandoned your post!"

"But they were all around me!"

"You're no use to us here. Go back to the wagons."

"They'll kill me!"

He lifted his rifle. "I'll give you to the count of five to obey your command! Go back to camp!"

At the count of three Moore sprang to his feet and started to run. He ran long-legged and the downhill helped him. But as he came to the top of an exposed place several guns cracked, and he went down. Wounded, he tried to crawl, but they kept shooting until he lay still; the guns kept on at regular intervals, using him for target practice, and each time a bullet thudded home his limp body trembled.

Garside turned and looked around as if for a challenge, and getting none said to Linstrom:

"Linstrom, you're a good shot. I want you to get uphill to those fallen logs. Some brave will be crawling out to get his scalp and when he does I want him shot in the guts. Hit him low and leave him alive."

"If I get one you want him to just crawl away?"

"That's exactly what I want, and as for you others, I don't want any putting him out of his misery. I want them shot in the groin if possible. I don't want 'em killed. We'll never kill all these Indians, and a dead one don't bother 'em. A dead one lies out there nice and still and they get to howling for revenge. It puts a different color on it when they get 'em back screaming with the piss flowing out of 'em." He got to laughing about it. Most of the men had never seen him show amusement, aside for a tight smile, but the picture he drew made him laugh until there was moisture to be wiped from the corners of his eyes. "Ah, yes, we might as well put 'em to work for us."

The fight went on—a series of sallies and retreats, of sniping at long range. Hours passed and it started to snow. A stormy twilight was gathering.

"Injuns never attack at night," someone said. "Ain't that true? Haven't you heard that? It has something to do with their religion."

"Tell McCoy that," said Fisher.

"Yes, tell me that," he said, touching his shattered face.

"What are we waiting for?"

Dennis said confidentially, "The Major had it in mind to set up a sort of half-way fort here to hold the ground so the train could pass. The only good spot is above on that little knoll with the trees, but how could he get the wagon there?"

It was true—Indians, additional bands of tens and dozens, kept passing along the ridge out of range and they could strike any such attempt with the advantage of altitude. The men kept looking at Garside to see what he would do—hole up for the night, wait for dark and retreat, or, the thing they all dreaded, make a try to establish the half-way post.

It became obvious by the voices and occasional gunfire that the Indian force was building. They might hold out against the original twenty or thirty, but there were double or triple that number in the brush, while groups of hard-traveled-looking horsemen kept appearing around the southwest flank of the ridge, stopping as men will do to get a first look, and then riding out of view.

Looking big-jawed and mean, bitter from the acceptance of defeat, Garside said, "Get ready, we're pulling back."

"To the train?"

"Yes, to the train."

"Hitch the mules, Major?" asked Tunis.

"No, leave the wagon."

"How about all this stuff."

"Take what we can. Get all the powder and ball. See if there's some way of mounting the swivel gun on one of the mules. Save the harness, we're not losing that."

Cox asked, "How about poor Veach? We can't take him belly over a horse. He's got to have the wagon."

"We're leaving the wagon."

"But how . . . ?"

"You said we can't take him belly over a horse. And we're leaving the wagon."

"We can't leave him here like this!"

"Right. He's your friend. You know what the Indians would do to him."

"But good God . . ."

"You have a gun, don't you?"

"I'm willing to carry him on my back."

"Nobody's carrying anybody on their backs. Put him out of his misery, he can't live anyhow."

Cox looked sick, but he left, and after a while there was a single report of a gun—the dead sound of it held close to a yielding object—and everyone stiffened. Save for Garside who seemed to pay no attention, who was making a last survey of the route out, ordering men, giving each his position and task, having the wagon filled with pitch wood and juniper to be set afire.

"Ready?" he asked in the snowy, settling darkness.

"All ready," said Abel.

"Listen, now. It's about dark enough. The flames will blind them until we can get past the crossing. Don't run! Do you hear that? The first man who spurs his horse had better keep right on going, because when I catch him I'll kill him."

He let that sink in. It was very quiet and they could hear the soft rattle of snow pellets falling among the dry hanging leaves.

He then called roll, had a final appraisal, ordered them down to the creek, and set fire to the wagon. He came and waited, and McCoy could hear the nostril-sound of his breathing in the dark. The wagon was a long time starting to burn. There was a great deal of smoke, then the flames rose with a bright hissing and an odor like turpentine. Indian voices on all sides set up a victory shouting, each group thinking another responsible, and one could hear the crack of rifles and the whisk of arrows as they crept down to the edge of firelight. The column moved quietly. They came to the crossing and rode past without drawing a shot. They rode on and on and came within the actual smell and horse-snort of Indians without drawing a shot, their identity lost in the darkness. At last they spotted the fires of the wagon camp, and a sentry hailed them.

Everyone was down to see them come in. The shooting had been heard and there had been a rescue group formed. Word went around that Moore and Veach had been killed. McCoy saw Bethel Hulbush looking at him. He had the impression that she was watching for him particularly, and he was suddenly glad to be home, and glad he was not off north somewhere running for Montana.

Garside closed himself in his wagon. He was in a brutal mood. He had lost a wagon worth seventy dollars in North Platte and twice that in the gold camps. He noticed as he rode in that his horse, his favorite dapple gelding, Abelard, was limping, and he had stopped to supervise while a hoop-steel arrowhead was removed from his thigh. He had given orders to pack the wound with a salt-pork poultice, but it was in the muscle where a knot might develop giving Abelard a permanent limp.

He poured a brandy and cursed his luck. The maps had all been wrong, or else Denker had guided him up the wrong valley. There was no one to turn to. They all hated him. He had seen it on their faces; their attitude in regards to Moore; their repugnance at the decision he had been forced to make in shooting Veach. Did it ever occur to them that he had done it for them as well as for himself? That if it hadn't been for a man able to make such decisions they might be lying out there dead? He had brought them back alive and had they come around to thank him? But that was man's ingratitude. He laughed bitterly. Even the Gileadeans were growing hostile and muttering against his leadership, now that their cattle had begun to die.

As he sat, he could look outside through the little isinglass window and see the campfires and falling snow. Everyone, even the poorest roustabout with the renegade wagons, had someone to talk to, eat with, complain to. But not him. He had nobody. Except in the late, secret hours, with Pet Denker.

Abel was outside talking to somebody. Abel was saying no, that Mist' Major was resting, but he heard the word "Hulbush," and thinking Bethel had sent for him went to the door.

It was Brother Samuel with word that Hulbush was "ill poorly" and wished to see him. Would he come?

"Directly," said Garside.

He had Abel shave him and bring a change of linen, and, hiding his fatigue—giving nobody the satisfaction of knowing that he was troubled by his setback in the pass—walked across the camp.

Bethel came to meet him, and he took hold of her hands.

"Your father . . . I came as soon as I could. How is he?"

"He's taken a bad cold. He asks to see you."

"Ah, Pray God, pray God," he said, pressing her hands.

She took him up the steps and through a canvas curtain which had been strung to keep some of the fore-and-aft wagon draft off the man's bed standing in a cleared place in the middle. A candle was burning. It shone across his face making him look sharp-beaked and skin-over-bones. With eyes closed, hands folded and beard carefully combed, he looked like a body waiting burial. He felt the tremble of the wagon under Garside's step and looked. His eyes were intense.

"Ah, Brother Garside! It is kind of you to come to me in these times which are so troublous! I understand the sorrow that overflows your heart and I would commiserate with you."

Garside controlled his expression. He looked sad and benign. He speculated whether the man was going to die shortly, and if so how well could he control his successor?

Hulbush said, "Your loss of Brother Moore and

Brother Veach must sorrow you deeply. It is my understanding that Brother Veach leaves a widow and several fatherless children in Colorado."

"Well, the Lord giveth and the Lord taketh away."

"Amen, Brother. And blessed is His spirit which walketh the earth, even in times of desolation."

"How do you feel, Brother Hulbush?"

"I will not live this winter out. I pray only to see my people arrived at their new home. Ah, then at last can I lie down in peace!"

"You'll see it out. Just make up your mind that, with *God's help,* you will do it. All of us get discouraged, Brother. We'd have reached our destination weeks ago but for a couple of accidents. And the weather. However, we will camp here yet a few days and everyone will feel better. Those Indians won't wait in the pass much longer, that's a certainty."

He did not seem to be listening. "I had a vision last night."

"Papa!" said Bethel trying to dissuade him, but he made a negative sign and went on:

"I was walking naked, there were no clothes on me, nor shoes nor hat, yet I was not ashamed for I was alone in the sight of God. Only my hair and beard were long, as one risen from his tomb. I walked and walked, and it seemed that I was on an endless plain. Not tree there was, nor flower, nor plant, nor dwelling. But then I met a man and knew him to be Brother Larkin—dead these twenty years—and I spoke to him. 'Where am I?' I asked, 'that all is desolation?' and he answered saying. 'You are in the new city of Gilead, which is called Garden City.' And I said, 'There is no city here for this is naught but desert.' Then we said and did other things, and they were nightmare things I dread to think about.

Ah, Brother, it was a portent and a warning. Today I try not to remember it for it fills me with desolation and I am sick at heart."

"It was a dream, Brother, and we all have them. Has that renegade been talking to you again?"

"What renegade?"

"McCoy."

"No, but he comes tonight."

Garside said deadfaced, "And how is it he comes tonight?"

"I have sent for him."

"For what purpose? He already told you that all of us would die and turn to cannibals. It seems to me that should be enough to sicken a Christian."

"I am sore in doubt. Don't believe I lack faith in you, Brother, yet so many look to me. I was told by Reverend Klinkke that there are some in the Gentile camp who talk of hurrying north to the settlements. It was my thought . . ."

"You mean that I am no longer your captain?"

"No, Brother Garside. Only . . ."

"Is it *yes* or is it *no*? If I'm your captain, then you will listen to me and not to those renegades."

"But Brother . . ."

"I ask you directly, Elder Hulbush! Do you choose me or McCoy?"

Beaten and tired, Hulbush said, "I choose thee, Brother."

"Then you will not listen to his poison tonight."

"No, I will not."

Garside experienced a recovery of spirits. After a day of defeat he saw his luck changing. Tomorrow it might turn warm, the snow vanish, and he would stage some lightning stroke against the Indians. He would return with a larger force and set up rifle pits at two of the points to command the midportion of the pass. Once in command of the high ground he could locate the Indians' main camp, draft every man able to aim a gun, descend on it, and destroy it. His mind teemed with plans and victory. He reached the Hulbush shoulder and pressed it.

"Brother! Can't you see that I stand to lose equally with you? Ah, how I have prayed! Yes on my knees, *prayed,* that some day your people could be my people. I have even dared to hope for something else. Can't you guess what I am talking about?" He turned to the girl. "Bethel! Take my hand. Please. Brother Hulbush, I wish to marry your daughter. I wish to be your son. I wish . . . I can say *we?*" he looked at her. There was no negation in her eyes. "*We* wish to face this great new land together. Bethel and I. For, while it is indeed evening for you, it is morning for us, Brother Hulbush. It is our hope that our seed will multiply to settle this great, new country. Your grandchildren, Brother. To occupy the land, and win it, and make it blossom."

He was somewhat carried away by himself. And there was a genuine tremble in his voice. He saw he had been so very effective that Hulbush raised himself to his elbows.

Looking from Garside to his daughter he said, "Do I hear right? Oh, praise God, this is what I have dreamed of. Daughter, is it also your wish?" She did not answer, but without taking her hands from Garside's she lowered her eyes, and her breathing showed her excitement. "You do wish this. Then praise Almighty God I will lie down to my everlasting rest knowing that my people will be cared for."

"You're not going to die!" she said.

But he brushed the idea away; he indicated he would be glad to die, to lie down his burden at last, that nothing could touch him now.

"My son," he said to Garside, "long ago a great prophet named Abraham Jepson rose among our people in their darkest hour and led them from the sin and wickedness of Pennsylvania into Ohio and thence to the green fields of Indiana. But in his dying vision he saw that the end of our wandering was not yet; that one day we would be driven thence, and on to the West where after great hardships—and wandering for forty days and forty nights, and four times forty—a new prophet would arise and we were to follow him. Surely that prophecy is now being fulfilled. And now indeed my dreaming vision has become plain to me. I see now that the desert I walked on was truly but a field waiting the seed in order to bloom with abundance—the seeds of wheat and of corn and the seed which springeth from your loins. Ah, I will sleep tonight knowing you are to remain with my people and will sire my grandchildren."

"Amen!" said Garside, his voice shaking with a genuine emotion. "Amen, as the Lord speaketh unto thee, Brother, so also He speaketh unto me!"

True to his promise, Elder Hulbush refused to see McCoy after sending for him.

"But I'm McCoy," he said to the Gileadean sentry. "The Elder sent for me."

He kept a gun ready. "Nobody can see the Elder. He is sick."

"Send and ask."

But the sentry was dogged, and McCoy too tired to fight about it. He was cold, and his face had taken to aching. But as he turned away, something occurred to him and he asked, "Is Garside still with him?"

Taken by surprise the sentry said, "About one hand since."

The Gileadeans had no clocks and measured time by the sun, its movement across one outsretched palm being, McCoy supposed, about fifteen minutes.

"So that's why he changed his mind!"

The sentry merely stood with the gun. He was stolid as McCoy's old muley packhorse. A dull, clodlike people, the Gileadeans. What was there about the ultra-faithful which made them so uninteresting? Aside from Bethel, Zuph, Klinkke, and a couple more he found them a repellent lot. He turned away, and some movement attracted his attention to the wagons.

It was Bethel. She was dressed like all the Gileadean women, so it had been some characteristic gesture of grace which informed him. She was gone, but he knew, with anticipation that grew to a pleasurable anguish, that she was going the long way around to meet him unseen. He started through a line of trees which separated the two parts of the wagon camp, when she called to him.

"Brother McCoy!"

She did not wish to come into view of the sentry. She waited and he went to her.

"I'm sorry," she said. "I couldn't do a thing. He promised to talk to you, and then the Major came and made an issue of it."

"What was it he wanted?"

"Papa?"

"Yes."

"He had a dream. It was terrible. He woke me up last night and I sat with him for hours. He's so sick with worry. He never wanted to lead. He knew he wasn't a prophet. There was just no one else. In Indiana we were against the war, and they burned our barns, calling us Copperheads. I have two brothers. Or *had.* They left home. My father quarreled with them, and they never wrote. He loved them so. Zodok and Manessah. We never mention them—I know what pain it gives him— but I hear him saying their names in his sleep."

He wanted to say something that would lighten her burdens, but the things which came to his mind were too ordinary. He touched her shoulder and was surprised when she came to him. The feel of her body under the voluminous garments caused him to forget all about the Elder, Zodok, and Manessah.

"I'll never do anything that will hurt him again," she said.

He knew something had happened, something besides his illness and the troubles of leading.

"I wish I could help."

"It could only make it worse! That's why you mustn't see him."

"How could I make it worse? What are you trying to do, fight your way through this pass to reach a nowhere? If you rolled for Montana at least you'd have a goal—towns, supplies. Do you know what it will be like on that windswept shoulder of nothing when the thermometer gets down to fifty below? Or don't you people believe in thermometers? It gets so cold that every creek freezes solid to the bottom, and the bottom freezes under that. You'll see weeks pass and not a living movement in all the land. Even the smoke will hang solid in the air. I've seen it so cold that bullets stick in the barrels of guns and you have to heat them in the fire, if you have one, and drive them out with a ramrod."

She cried, "And what's to be gained by telling him

such things?"

"Even if they're true?"

"We can't follow two leaders. We've chosen to follow Major Garside."

It was true. You had to choose one leader and stick with him. And deep down he knew that Garside in his way was one hell of a leader. He turned to go, but he knew she did not want him to go. In the dark, by silhouette, he could see the curve of her cheek and nose, and the fine strength of her brow. She was beautiful; not the beauty that stopped a person at first glance, but the sort which grew on you and became a thing of being, and doing, and things wanted—the beauty that came from inside.

"They want me to lead them to Montana," he said, meaning the independent wagons.

"I know."

"Come with us. Klinkke wants to come with us."

"But he won't. He'll do what Papa says."

"You talk with him. Reason with him. Don't *you* want to go?"

She wouldn't answer.

"Don't you?"

"No, no. I want you to go. I never want to see you again! It's the only way."

She kissed him. For a few seconds she was in his arms, then she pulled away and ran.

"Bethel!" He followed. "Bethel!" but she did not turn, and the sentry, gun up, was looking their way.

It warmed in the morning and the snow started to thaw. The grass clumps made watery circles all across the flat. Then, in a matter of minutes, the south breeze swung around northeast and blew frigid, freezing the grass in

111

transparent circles of ice. It kept snowing—a soft powder—but the ice remained as a glass-hard coating which broke under the hoofs and cut the animals when they attempted to paw for feed, and they left their tracks ringed pink from blood.

At midnight, seeing the state of things, and with enough experience with northern winters, Doc got up and went quietly from one independent wagon to the next, waking the sleepers and telling them to get up and gather the bark of the sweet cottonwood for emergency feed before the "Hogall" Gileadeans got in their licks; by dawn, there remained only a small grove of choice trees across the creek. A fight developed over these; there was some long-range shooting, but both sides retired, the trees unstripped.

A scouting party left at noon and reached the main ridge. They ran into only an ineffectual scatter of shots, a rock-splinter wound in the rump of one horse, but returned with the report that Indians, in a force of at least four hundred, held the narrows. Garside's thermometer read one degree above zero, and he predicted the Indians would leave for winter quarters, it was only a matter of waiting them out. But next day they were still there, and that night they grew so bold as to creep up and attack from long range one group of wagons and, using the diversion, to charge through the other end of camp, running off seven of the Gileadeans' mules. Later Brother Gove failed to return to his wagon and in the morning he was found naked, gutted, and scalped with a dozen arrows driven through him.

Reverend Klinkke conducted the service: "We look unto you, O Jehovah, and ask hast Thou abandoned us on this snowy desert?" Klinkke intoned. "We ask, O Jehovah, that You, who are all powerful, send us a sign

112

or a portent, as Thou did in the olden times, that we may follow it forth from this wilderness."

The words, Garside felt, were aimed at himself, but he remained with his head bowed and the north wind stirring his hair.

"O, Mighty Jehovah, send us a man to lead us in this perilous time!" cried Klinkke.

"You didn't need to say it in prayer, Reverend," said Garside walking to him while the frozen clods were being shoveled. "If you have some objection to the way I'm guiding this train, be man enough to say it to my face."

"Are we sitting here to starve?" asked Klinkke.

"Of course not. I have been in prayer that the weather would break. Otherwise, by tomorrow, we leave."

"For where?"

"I look, like you, to heaven for a portent."

The weather did not break. It became so cold that the ice had to be chopped from the waterholes. That evening, Garside called a meeting of all the wagoners and spoke:

"I have no doubt we could reach Garden City, if not by this route, then by turning back to the Portuguese Flats which would now be frozen and passable. However, supplies are getting low, and it would be difficult to build suitable shelters with snow on the ground. One must consider the women and the little ones. I have decided to take the shortcut to Fort T. M. Hunter. Over the mountains. The snow there will be heavier, but without this ice crust. My scouts report grass in some of the elk meadows to be waist-deep. It will be difficult, but short. On the other hand there is little chance we will have trouble with these hostiles. Mr. Denker and his scouts will leave to explore a trail tonight. We will follow as soon after dawn as we can

113

get rolling. I know you will be disappointed at this decision, but it was the only one your commander could decently make in consideration of the women and children who otherwise might be made to suffer."

Then he strode leather-faced to his wagon, up the steps, and through the door which he closed behind him.

CHAPTER 4

THE MEN WHO HAD GATHERED AT KAVANAUGH'S wagon stopped talking when Bigfoot Charlie Denker came up carrying a tin cup for a measure of wheat wine.

"It was quite a joke on you fellows, wanting to bust off for Montana, and here all the while the Major was planning something of the same thing."

Kavanaugh waited for him to hand over a quarter, his credit being long since exhausted.

"I'd buy for you fellows," he said, paying, drinking and burping, "but I'm short onto cash. You don't need to think I made any money out of this proposition. No sir, all the wagon fees Garside puts in his own pocket strictly, and he even talked me into acting as a guide for his train free of charge. Dinked me out of my townsite and road corporation, too. In fact, I'm getting my gut mighty full of that fellow, if you know what I mean."

It occurred to McCoy, who had joined the group, that he wanted to get them to talk so he could carry information back to Garside. Perhaps he wanted to know if they were making new plans now that the destination was Fort Hunter. Denker motioned him to one side.

"These fellows," he indicated Kavanaugh and the rest, "they don't trust me. They got me pegged as the

114

Major's man. On the other hand, the Mormons—Gileadeans, whatever they are—they distrust me, too. They know I'm a Roman Catholic. Well, it's true. I had no more religion than a hog, but a Jesuit irrigated me when I took my squaw. We named our kids Ignatius, Teresa, Peter, John, Gregory, Luke after popes, saints. So those bastardly Gileadeans hate my guts. And the feeling is both ways. Granted, you might look at 'em different, the way they favored you, took you in and put you to bed. And in the Hulbush wagon, no less! Maybe that pretty Hulbush gal got in and warmed it for you."

He made a movement causing Denker to retreat. "Oh-ho! No offense intended. I don't know and I don't want to know. If she got in under the covers with you it's none of my affair. Only reason I mentioned it was because it would explain a couple of things. I mean, the way Garside went for you."

He waited, controlling his annoyance, wondering what it was Denker wanted. Because the man was not stupid. He was filthy, and obscene, and a killer, but he was not dull. He had the mind of a clever animal.

"You want to wed up with that Gileadean girl? Do you? You don't want *him* sleeping with her, anyhow, Right! Well, we're on the same side. You set that down in your book and don't you forget it. And I'd say to seal it with another snort of this wine if I hadn't left all but a double-shilling in my money bag."

McCoy bought him the drink. Denker did not touch it—he allowed he'd have it after supper—and said again in private: "I don't want to go into this right now, but don't forget what I said about us being on the same side."

Denker carried the wine back to his camp, careful not to spill a single drop. It was bubbly and had the taste of yeast, but it warmed his gullet, and gave the buckled-up feeling so needed by a man of his years, tired and hungry, with winter coming on.

Pet was working around the fire, putting things in a stewpot. It was the way her mother, who was a Blood Blackfoot, had taught her to cook. Everything went in—potatoes, camas roots, beef, buffalo, rabbit, prairie chicken—even dog when the times were tough, or when some cur was making himself a pest around the camp—but not too much liquid, or otherwise the leftover couldn't be carried. When you were on the trail it was important that the stew solidify as soon as it got cold, then you could sling the pot on a packhorse and have spooning grease when you made a stop. God, how packhorses hated a stewpot. It knocked against their sides and boomed like a bell and caught in the brush and always seemed to make the load lopsided. One time he was guiding for some Englishmen over in Dakotah who had come to hunt buffalo, and they had a real gaunt old gelding that was about the tallest horse he ever saw—it must have been well over eighteen hands high—and one of them had the idea to balance the stewpot by hanging it under its belly, and it got urinated in. It was the funniest thing Denker ever saw, and he hadn't said a thing, just swore off stew for a couple of days. Yes, those were the good times, guiding and traveling with his squaw. He used to trade whisky for skins and take her along. She knew so many little tricks of making out. For example, she took extra moccasins and made them serve double by packing pemmican in them. The pemmican would solidify like cement—you'd break a bowie trying to pry it out—only when you needed new moccasins you just tossed them in the pot, the pemmican turned to rich gravy, and you fished out the moccasins steaming and slick and put them on and they shrank right down to the size of your hoof. Just another proof of how a white man, wanting to live in the country, couldn't do better than get himself a good squaw. But it was important to get himself a good one. However, you could say the same about horses or anything else.

Pet, he was thinking, would make somebody a damn good squaw. She could do anything a Blackfoot could, and, give her a chance, she could make out with any white woman. And he didn't mean these old mares that came along with the emigrant wagons, he meant the ones all laced and perfumed like they had for the officers at the army posts.

He knew well enough that Garside had made Pet his squaw already. He didn't know exactly how long it had been going on, but one night he'd been lying there in the dark, and Garside came walking over to get in the robes with her. He had been coming quiet, but in a hurry, trembling and eager like a stallion off the green grass, and Denker just laid there and listened. Well, whatever happened Pet could never say that she hadn't had it from a real man, and that was a consideration not to be dismissed lightly. There were plenty of women raised in the lap of luxury unable to say the same thing, if the truth was known, and felt cheated by life on account of it. Thinking of Pet and Garside made him remember his own younger days among the squaws of the Indian camps when you could buy just anything for a cut pint of whisky. "That's how it is," he muttered. "When you're young you have it and when you're old you think about it, and one day you're over the hill and in the ground." With a passing chill be thought of the state of his soul. But he reassured himself knowing that

117

everything he'd done was for his family—to get a little money, horses, property, and leave them something less than destitute.

Pet worked around the stewpot, rather withdrawn and somber. She had the look about the face that his wife always got when she was a couple or three months pregnant. It meant that Garside must have got to her almost as soon as they left Soda Junction. He wouldn't want to marry her. She was a squaw and that was understandable. Denker felt no outrage, but he aimed to get her her rights. There were several ways of doing this, depending. Easiest and direct would be just kill him and take over all property in Pet's name, common law, unborn child, etc. Denker was good at arithmetic which he did by Indian abacus, with pebbles, and he had several times appraised Garside's outfit—wagons, horses, mules, supplies—and came up with something over $6,800, gold-camp valuation. Also, it was fairly certain he had some cash or negotiables in his wagon. However, he did not wish to act too soon. There was such a thing as killing the goose, which laid the golden egg.

"That smells like gut stew," said Denker over the pot. "What you got in there?"

"Horse meat," said Pet.

"Good God, have we come down to that? Was it a fallen one?"

"Broken leg."

"Well, that's just as bad, or worse. You work hell out of a horse, then you kill him; it's the toughest meat in the world. I'd rather have a fallen one. You have a fallen horse, he gives up, he relaxes a little. That looks like neck meat. Who marked shares on that horse— Garside? You'd think he'd have something better than neck meat for us, everything considered." He looked steadily at Pet's abdomen as he said it, but she gave no sign of understanding. "Who got the heart, tongue, and liver? The Holy Rollers? Who got the loin meat? Did he take that to Hulbush?"

She kept pulling pieces of steaming flesh from the pot, laying them on a slab of wood, and pounding them with a club. By such work, pounding and boiling, all the flesh, the bone, even the gristle would be reduced to a sort of gritty gruel—it was one of the things she had learned from her mother.

Garside was thinking of Pet also. He sat in his wagon alone thinking that if they went to Fort Hunter, and wintered there, he might not have the chance of sending her on to Yellowstone City. Her condition would become obvious and it would call for an explanation. He had to provide that.

"Abel," he said at the door, "will you fetch Mr. Halleck?"

"Dave!" he cried cordially when Halleck arrived. "Dave, come in, come in! Sorry I've been missing you lately. How about a brandy, Dave?"

"Oh, thanks, Henry." He was the only man who ever called Garside by his given name. Even Bethel, who was promised to be his wife, called him "Major." He seemed cautious, but anxious to please. It was not like Garside to send for him through simple friendship.

"Well, Dave! Is it a relief to have a decision at last? It is for me although I'll admit it's one hell of a disappointment to give up the road and townsite for the season. However, I've been thinking we can travel on to the Yellowstone and swing back down from the north as soon as the roads clear, and be just about as far ahead.

And incidentally, Dave, I've been meaning to make over an interest in this thing to you. Townsite, road, everything. You've been practically a partner of mine, Dave, and I say it's high time that fact was recognized in some concrete manner."

"Thanks!"

"By the way, did you notice Denker was visiting me?"

He shook his head.

"Last night. He was right here at this wagon, Dave. He was talking about you. Came to me because we were relatives. You must be able to guess why."

"No. I . . ."

"Ah, now, Dave! He wants to know your intentions in regards to his daughter!"

There was a slight reaction, a flinch, but the redhead controlled it, "My intentions?"

"Yes! We all know how you feel toward her. She's a real pretty girl, Dave. And this is the West. We don't think twice about Indian blood here."

"What are you getting at?" he asked nervously.

"Dave, I've been observing things. That girl is *waiting* for you. He as much as said so. Her own father. He'll go out on scout tonight, so why don't you call on her?"

He stood, looking at Garside, and his fingers trembled holding the glass. "You mean she's ready to sleep with me?" he asked in a tight voice.

"Well, now, that's hitting the spike a little more than I intended. I can't tell you to *do* such a thing. It's up to you . . . and to her. However, *if* you do there's a responsibility involved. I mean, it's a custom of the country for her to be then regarded as your wife. I'd want you to do the right thing, Dave."

"She never had a second look for me."

Garside knew by his tone that all was well, he suspected nothing; or if he suspected he was still willing to overlook it. He was in love, stupidly in love, with the half-breed girl.

"But, Dave! She's part Indian. She thinks like an Indian. When an Indian girl has her blanket spread for a certain man she pretends she doesn't even know he's alive. Indian girls will walk off when he comes, turn their backs on him. Then a relative comes around, or a friend, and they talk to a friend of the man, and that's how the arrangement is made. Tonight, do as I say. Wait for Denker to leave and call on her. Go ahead, Dave! Give it a try!"

After two days of relatively easy travel, the road to the Big Horns entered a deep, wooded gulch and became a hell of rocks and sidehills. They were four days getting as many miles with as high as six-span teams needed to pull some of the steep banks which everywhere closed the creek. McCoy had charge of a jerkline team since before dawn, helping on wagon after another, but at last he was able to give over his job to young Billy Tucker and walk forward to where Kavanaugh's wagon had stopped in a cluster of rock pine, and went to sleep inside on the floor.

He woke up lying in a lurching wagon, and it was dark. Someone was outside cursing and using his weight on one of the wheels. The four-horse team kept trying, but each time, at the very apex, their footing would fail, stones rolled under the snow, and they would fall back again. He stood holding to the sides until the wagon came to rest in a crush of evergreens, and climbed out. He immediately sank to the thighs in snow. Aldo Rimmel was helping at the wheel and Kavanaugh driving. Above and a couple hundred yards away some fires were blazing. Steep little ridge summits rose on both sides. The trees looked very pointed and perfect against a background of snow. Overhead some cold stars were out, but no moon.

He added his weight and the teams, with a final, lunging struggle, made it. They rolled on to the place where Chuck Rimmel was building a fire. Other camps were scattered along the gulch for half a mile, in flats and tiny clearings, a lack of cohesion which indicated the danger of Indians was far past.

He helped with the unhitching and went to the fire carrying his tin plate for supper. It was one of the lucky camps, having Mrs. Kavanaugh for cook. She could manage even horse meat and dried turnips into something palatable, and for the last couple of days there had been elk, a cow-animal shot and kept away from the meat wagon where, like as not, it would have been divided so all the better parts went to the Gileadeans.

After the meal was over and the beds were being made each one to the person's own fancy, in the wagons, or outside beneath the snow—Joe Reid's old black dog raised a commotion which was generally reserved for Indians, so Kavanaugh took his pistol and went to investigate. He found Pet Denker hiding in the bushes, her face lopsided from a beating. She was very frightened and might have run but for the fact that the Rimmels had come around behind her, so she let Mrs. Kavanaugh take her inside the wagon. In a little while Mrs. Kavanaugh came outside and motioned for McCoy.

"She seems to be talking Injun. I can't understand half what she says. You claim to know most everything;

come in and see what you can make out."

He did, and found Pet cowering in the candlelight. Her face was swollen, with remnants of blood around her nostrils and the sides of her mouth. Her cheeks looked as if they bad been gouged by a rasping file. Apparently she had been knocked into brush, or the deadwood.

"Who beat you?" he asked. "Was it Garside? You don't need to be afraid. We won't let him take you. Was it Garside?"

"No! Not Major. He my husband."

"*Garside* your husband?"

"Yes!"

"I heard it was Halleck."

"No, Major my husband."

"Why didn't you go to him?"

"Now, hold on," said Mrs. Kavanaugh. "We're not sending this poor thing to . . ."

"Be quiet a minute. Why did you come here if Major is your husband? I understood Dave Halleck was your husband. He was passing a bottle around, saying he was your husband."

"Yes."

"What do you mean *yes*? You mean both of them are your husbands?"

"Yes."

"Well, I'll be . . ." said Mrs. Kavanaugh. "Do you hear that? They're sharing her between 'em."

"Did Dave Halleck beat you?"

She nodded.

McCoy couldn't imagine Dave doing it.

"That redheaded sneak," said Mrs. Kavanaugh. "A fine excuse for a man. Always around kissing Garside's hindside!"

"Say, that was pretty good!" said Kavanaugh, at the

123

endgate.

"Shut up! She's scared and no more'n a child. Her dirty old father had something to do with all this if you want my opinion. You don't need to be scared of anybody as long as I'm around, honey. I got a shotgun loaded with buck, and I can use it. You don't need to be scared of your paw, or Garside, or Halleck, or anybody. Because I'll turn 'em so the hair side's in."

She pushed McCoy through the door and closed it. From outside their shadows could be seen distorted against the canvas. She was undressing the girl.

"How is she, Maw?" asked Kavanaugh.

"Keep your nose out of here. She's been kicked all around the ribs low down something terrible. Why, nothing but a ragin' animal would do a thing like that."

A man rode up and stopped. They knew he was looking and listening. Finally he came on into the firelight. The man was Garside.

"Did that girl come here?" he asked.

"What girl?" asked Kavanaugh.

"Wait a second," said McCoy. He motioned Kavanaugh back. "Yes, she came here."

"Is she in the wagon?"

"Yes."

"Tell her to come out."

When nobody moved to comply he dismounted and started for the rear door. Mrs. Kavanaugh had been listening and met him with an old eight-gauge shotgun.

"I came for that girl, Mrs. Kavanaugh."

"You're not taking her. You come one step closer and I'll shoot you in the belly and blow your backbone out."

"Maw!" said Kavanaugh.

"Stay clear of this! This is between the Major and myself." She addressed Garside, "What do you want

124

with her?"

"I want to take her back to her father. She's Indian, and they don't look at things like we do. I've found out we have to treat her and her brother both like Indians, and respect their ways."

"That may be so, but as far as I'm concerned she's just a scared girl, not much more'n a child, and she came to me for help. She's been beat, do you know that?"

"I'm here to learn the truth of that, Mrs. Kavanaugh."

"I'll tell you the truth of it. It was that stinking, sneaking redheaded cousin of yours, Dave Halleck."

"She said that?"

"Yes!"

"Did she say where Dave was?"

"No."

He decided not to challenge Mrs. Kavanaugh and her eight-gauge. He could do that without loss of face because he was a military man and she was a woman. He bowed to her, turned and said to McCoy. "If you let that girl go one step from here before I get back, I'll bring my men up here and riddle this camp with gunfire. I'll burn you out, every wagon in this group, and those of you still alive will be on foot starving for the wolves. I am leaving her here with that clear understanding."

They all watched in silence as he mounted and rode away.

"You make your understanding and I make mine," Mrs. Kavanaugh muttered at his back, "but I'm not leaving her go till I'm well satisfied she'll be safe. In the meantime, I'm unclothing this poor girl, and making a complete examination. If you want my opinion she's had too much attention from male critters already."

✧✧✧

Dave Halleck had always been as loyal to Garside as it was possible for a man to be. He called himself a cousin, though actually he was only a cousin of the Major's first wife. He had served as Garside's helper and minor partner, often as not unpaid. He was hard-working, and dependable. He was not brave, but nobody called him a coward, either. He was as good a man as his natural abilities would permit. In a mild way, he was popular. His loyalty for Garside was understood, so nobody took him much in their confidence, but they did not dislike him. As they did not gossip about the Major in his presence, he was one of the few people on the train who had not heard about his night visits to Pet Denker. There were a few broad innuendos, nothing more. Had anyone except Garside guessed that Halleck himself had more than a normal yearning for the girl, no doubt the innuendos would have increased.

For Dave Halleck had from his first glimpse been taken by Pet Denker. She was not pretty—in fact by Illinois-blonde standards she would seem coarse and flat featured—but there was something about her, a strong grace in her movements, and a contour of legs, hips, and abdomen under her blanket garb, that drew him almost against his will, and filled him with warm imaginings.

However, the girl appeared scarcely aware of his existence. She seemed only interested in Garside. Dave could not help noticing the quick excitement in her manner whenever his cousin came around. Garside, however, seemed to make a point of ignoring the girl. He was obviously only interested in Bethel Hulbush. Almost every night, freshly shaved and changed, he went to the Gileadean camp. True, there had been times when he had come looking for the Major on some emergency and found his bed in the wagon unoccupied,

126

but Abel always had a ready explanation, and when, once he saw him coming at dawn from the brush of Denker's camp he immediately dismissed any suspicion that he had been to her bed. When Pet commenced to show a placid content in Garside's presence, quite a change from her previous excitement, he felt a budding of hope. Then Garside had sent for him, told him that he was the man after all, that her ignoring him was just an Indian's way, and he could see how blind he had been all along. If there remained any doubt it was erased when he visited her bed that night and found her waiting. Yes, she seemed to be expecting him, receiving him without a word, with a strong, dark competence.

Several nights passed, they were in the mountains, and he went to bed with her very tired after all day with the wagons; then he woke up, the moon shining, and found her sitting in bed stroking her abdomen. He sensed that she was many weeks pregnant.

"By Garside?" he demanded, suddenly rising in jealousy and anger.

She made no answer.

"It's Garside's." When still she made no sign of yes or no he stilled the shake in his voice and became clever. "He told me. Didn't you think I knew?"

"No-no, the baby is yours!" She seemed frightened, and looked around as if Garside might be listening.

"He told you to tell me that."

There was no need to force her admission.

"He told you to sleep with me!"

She did not answer. He had to get away and have a chance to think. He knew he had to do something, but he didn't know what. It occurred to him that he ought to kill Garside, but he knew he was utterly unable to do so. He was so long subservient to Garside that it had

127

become a fixed condition of his being, he could not even imagine shooting him in the back.

He got up and rode until dawn. He was in an unfamiliar country, among rocks and pines. He turned back, following his trail and in the afternoon sighted the wagon train. He had not eaten since the day before, but he was not hungry, and he felt as if he had a fever. He followed after the train. He kept watch of Pet who went on the same as always, riding her undersize, dog-gentle horse and managing her father's pack-string. He sat on a rock point above and watched her make camp in the twilight, and move around, cooking supper as usual. When he did not come, she ate, and covered the fire for morning, then all was still. She was in bed. He rode down and found her.

It was then he beat her, not severely at first, only to make her talk and admit what he knew was the truth; then furiously, unreasoning because she would not utter a word, or a whimper. She crawled away and he stripped her dress up to her shoulders and drove his foot to her naked body. He followed her, on and on, across the snow and through juniper and rocks until he cornered her, and there, standing, using a tree trunk for leverage, he kicked at her abdomen, wishing to destroy Garside's seed which was growing inside her. Only then, when she saw that this treasured thing might be injured did she fight back, get away, and run through the snow.

Halleck went back to his horse and rode. He had no destination. After a time he realized someone was following him. The moon was up, making the little mountain clearing almost like day. His horse stopped. Garside called, "Dave?"

He rode into the moonlight. "Dave? Oh, there you

are. What's the matter? What happened between you and Pet?"

Halleck looked at him and it came to him in a bitter flood how much loyalty he'd given this man—often without pay, always without question.

"What's the trouble? Out with it, Dave!"

"Were you going to make that Gileadean girl think it was my kid? Was that why you turned her over to me? You thought I'd think it was mine coming along too soon?"

He did not deny it. He sat and regarded Halleck quietly. "Well, things like that happen. I'll provide for the kid after it's born. There's only the three of us know, Dave. It still won't be a bad thing for you."

"No!" And suddenly, suicidally, he discarded all his fear. "To hell with you. I'll not go on living with her. And I don't claim the kid."

He made his tired horse move. He started around Garside to get back on the trail toward camp.

"Where you going, Dave?"

He had to stop as Garside blocked him. He was looking down the barrel of a rifle. Garside had been carrying it close to the side of his horse in his left hand. Just as suddenly, there was no more revolt in him. In terror he wanted to live. He wanted to take back everything he had said, agree to anything, anything Garside might ask.

"I didn't mean it!" he cried.

"No, Dave."

"Please, oh God, please . . ."

"Sorry, Dave. You can see I'd never feel right about you."

"No, no!"

In sick terror he half leaped, half fell from his horse.

129

He back-peddled through the snow until his boots tangled some dead buried boughs, and he fell. He sat looking up in sick, slack terror at the gun which was aimed at him. He tried to get up.

"No! Henry, Henry, Henry . . ."

"Take it like a man!" said Garside.

But he could not stop calling Garside's name as the gun exploded, and he was hit as by a thousand clubs—a crash and ringing and lights trailing away with the bursting multitude of thoughts to the darkness he knew was forever.

The single gunshot pounded around the icy hills, and Garside sat alone. Halleck was doubled over, looking peculiarly small and out of joint, in the snow. After a while, when there was no responding sound to the gunshot, Garside got down, thrust a boot under his ribs and lifted him so he would dump over in a different position. His eyes were slitted open, and the eyeballs had no more life than cold oysters. It was snowing gently. The flakes melted when they touched his skin, but after a while they gathered without melting. No one appeared from down the trail. No one would. The shot would go unnoticed. It kept snowing, clotting across Halleck's face, and turning his clothes to gray. The phenomenon of life and death struck him in that moment of solitude, and he thought how for so long— thirty-five, thirty-eight years—the warmth and breath and heartbeats, had been in this man uninterrupted, and now, at the squeeze of his finger, it was gone. More remarkable, how for thousands on thousands of years the quick and the warmth stretched back, through generation before generation, and now, after all the ages he was there at the instant when it flicked out. By morning the snow would quite cover him. No one would find him. Not for years. Or perhaps ever. Only the horse presented a problem. It was Garside's property, worth fifty dollars or more, with saddle and bridle extra. Then he thought, if he led him in who was going to question? He had found, often enough, that simple boldness was the safest way. And the most profitable.

He rode back, leading the horse and left it, bridle, saddle and all, telling the wrangler he had found it wandering, and made a joke about Dave, "the newlywed." He went again to Kavanaugh's wagon. All was quiet. A chilled sentry came forth and stood looking without making a challenge. Garside took no notice of him. Overcoming his fatigue by movements bigger and more positive than natural, he got down and rapped at the rickety slat door set half in the endgate and half in the bow-and-canvas top. Mrs. Kavanaugh, huge under the coverings of cotton flannel nightgowns, sweaters, and coats she put on nightly, came to peep out at him.

"Mrs. Kavanaugh!"

"You're talkin' to her. What do you want?"

"Is the girl still here?"

"Yes, o' course she's still here."

"I'm taking her back to her camp."

"Just like that, taking her back to camp. No is-she-well-enough. Nothing."

"I come!" said Pet behind her.

Mrs. Kavanaugh blocked her off and said, "I suppose you want to give that so-called husband another chance at her."

"No, Mrs. Kavanaugh. He's nowhere to be found."

"Well, lucky for him." She said to Pet, "You better go on back to bed, child. I don't think you should leave."

"I go," she insisted, sounding frightened.

Finally the big woman stood aside, making plain it

131

was against her better judgment, and said to Garside, "I hold you responsible."

"Thank you, Mrs. Kavanaugh. It always flatters me to be held responsible."

She kept watching in heavy truculence while the girl descended, got a stirrup, was helped up behind Garside, and rode off with him.

"Come back to bed, Maw," said her husband. "We're safe to be rid of her."

"Well, *he* better not mistreat her, either. She's awful scared of him. Just awful. I wouldn't be surprised if he was the one that kicked her."

"Maybe, but keep those ideas to yourself. I got all the trouble right now that I can handle."

Riding, Garside asked the girl behind him, "Did you tell them anything?"

"Nothing!"

"Did you tell them it was my baby?"

"No! You say not to!"

"But you told Dave."

"No. But he know. He *guess*!"

"Don't you ever admit it's not his."

"No!"

She was frightened, and that was all to the good.

"You taking me back to him?" she asked.

"No, I sent him away. You'll never see him again."

Pet's arms were around him as he rode. Her arms, and the smooth movement of her body under her robes, made him realize how tired he was, how the chill of the country had worked inside his bones, and he needed her.

They passed through timber which narrowed the trail, past other wagons, and up to the half-tent where she slept with Halleck, but with Halleck no longer. What a

132

fool he was, thought Garside. Dave could be warm in bed with her this minute instead of stiffening under the snow. That showed what could happen to a man who suddenly discovered pride and principles he couldn't afford. Then he saw fresh tracks, and tethered horses, and knew that Denker had returned.

"Pet?" said Denker. "Who's there? Oh, Major, you got Pet with you? What happened? The Missourians downhill say they heard Pet being beat up."

"She's all right now. Go back to bed."

"Well, a man has a right to worry about his own daughter. That son-of-a-bitch, Halleck! A fine hound of a husband you picked out for her! Where is he?"

"He's gone. He won't come back."

"He'd better not get back, because if I got my hands on him . . ."

"Go to bed," said Garside.

Denker plodded into the downhill bushes where his robes were poked under the brush and snow. He crawled in, twisting and grunting, without taking his boots off, or his hat. He had not removed his boots in a week, except to put some fresh grass in them. There was nothing like gray, wide-stem mountain grass to absorb sweat and keep the feet warm. He had not taken off his shirt or trousers for a month, and his underwear not since Soda Junction, but on a couple of the hottest afternoons he had laundered and bathed at the same time by getting in the creek with all his clothes on. It was a trick he'd learned long ago. You laundered everything without work, and your clothes dried on you soft and comfortable, a prime fit. He believed that in the winter bathing weakened a man and made him susceptible to disease, removing the insulation that kept

133

him warm, and leaving him the prey of lice. It was often proved that when a man was long enough sewed in his underwear the lice departed. Denker still scratched, but mostly from habit, and it was yet early in the season. When extolling his system, the wagoners affected to think lice avoided Denker because they could not stand his smell, but he scoffed at this. He was around himself all the time, he said, and hence ought to know better than anybody else what he smelled like. Lying in his robes, looking through snowy twigs at the night sky, he scratched by rubbing back and forth in the buffalo hair, and his thoughts turned to Halleck.

Halleck's horse was down at the rope corral, very hard ridden. He had removed none of his valuables. Everything he owned was either right there in the saddle pack or down at the dunnage wagon. Denker had inventoried him as well as he could in the event Pet was left a widow. Now she *was* a widow, carrying a kid that Garside would put forth to be Halleck's own. He had killed Halleck. It was almost too neat. It left him free and clear to marry the Holy Roller girl, and then what of poor Pet? And what of her father that had slaved for her and provided? Were they to put up with whatever Garside was willing to give? The thought made him uncomfortable so he rolled, and scratched, and rolled again.

"Well, by God," he muttered, rising to look over where Garside was in bed with his daughter, "she ain't a widow because there was no marriage ever pronounced. And as for it being Halleck's kid, I can come forward with some arithmetic."

But still he didn't know what procedure to take in getting Pet her rightful share. It was something he'd have to think about.

✧✧✧

134

Day after uncounted day the train moved higher and deeper into the mountains. No one had time to think of Halleck, or even realize he had vanished, as the wagons were dragged, often with rope tackle, from level to level, up the side of a terraced canyon. A storm caught them, and they waited it out as it rocked the wagons and flapped the canvas, and filled the interiors with a cold twinkle of snow.

It was easier after the drifts built up, giving shelter between the wagons and the walls of rock. Some of the men cut pine and laid it as crude roofs, and the stock was brought in for mutual warmth. At last the wind went down and the train dug itself out. Garside, mounted on his big gray, rode between the wagons and the edge, peering into the various camps and calling for the men he wanted: Bowers, McCoy, Aldo Rimmel, Blankenship; and the Gileadeans, Gaines, Sharpe and Ferrier. This group, climbing above, built a windlass using the spokes and axle of a wrecked wagon, and were able to pull the wagons, unloaded, up a near perpendicular slope. Meanwhile the cargoes went around a switchback route on teams turned to packhorses. So after two days several miles of nigh impassable going had been by-passed, and they traveled along a bleak slope, close now to the main wall of the mountains.

They had a view of the pass. It was a saddle between the slides and peaks. From close by the peaks were unexpectedly small, while the land away and below that seemed precipitous and vast.

"That son-of-a-bitch Denker took us up the wrong side," Kavanaugh said. "You can see the trail over there, a mile away."

The successive depressions of what might have been

a trail were plainly stamped along the side of the far slope, looping and zig-zagging to drop across the pass.

"Where's Denker now?" McCoy asked.

"I ain't seen him since we were on the windlass. He took one shift at that and got his bellyful. Claimed he had to scout ahead. If you want my guess he's took us here and left us, figuring he'll come back next spring for the remains."

They managed to move the wagons about two more miles. At that point fields of sandstone in blocks big as the wagon boxes lay ahead. It was a cirque with cliffs above and cliffs below. A game trail ran narrowly around the edge.

Denker returned and said that the trail was good enough, both there and down the Montana side, but the wagons would have to be knocked down and carried over. He remarked casually that it was only a five-and-a-half mile pack trip, camps could be set up on both sides, and two journeys made daily. It seemed to surprise him when there was bitterness toward him as a guide. "I never promised you a damn turnpike," he said.

Garside looked wolfish, and he was in a killing mood, but he made no comment. He issued commands to set up a temporary camp and sent out trail crews, wood crews, and hunters. The supplies went over first, the trail crew having set up a camp on the other side. After the wagons were knocked down it was found that the wheels could be converted into carts, and soon a snake road came into existence among the rocks. Only the wagon boxes proved truly difficult, but they got over on skids, some knocked down into sides, ends, and bottoms, and many never reassembled.

Denker described clear and easy going on the northeast side. What they found was a series of snowy slopes down which the vehicles could be lowered by rope tackle.

Denker all the while made himself comfortable in a secret camp below, only an occasional smoke hinting its position. When the first road crew found him he was finishing a mess of trout he had caught in a downcountry exploration. He regretted that there was not trout for everyone—he personally had never signed to hunt and fish for the commissary—but he gave directions to some teeming big beaver dams where "a ton of fish" could be got for the labor of a little chopping and seining. However the fishing party came back half-starved, no beaver dams having been found.

There was talk of hanging him, but no man had the energy after work and short rations to make the effort. One morning, after the portage had been in progress for ten days, Bowers' cousin, a forty-year-old bachelor named Mal Hall, was found dead in his robes. It was a case of overwork and starvation, and Bowers, a few minutes after discovering the body, and seeing some Gileadeans looking strong and well-fed leading mules laden with baskets of seed, charged into the trail waving a Navy and shouting, "You sons-of-bitches! *You* been eating fat and sharing none of yours."

He fired over their heads and into the ground before them, and the mules ran away. Later they were found stripped of their cargo, and when Garside came to the camp and demanded its return, the seed had already been ground Indian-style and baked into hoecakes.

A good third of the train was discarded; several of the emigrants, despairing of getting wagons moved—or deeming them too old and broken to be worth the work—merely took what was best, fashioned harness into packsaddle equipment, and went with new freedom and mobility. But most of the wagons were reassembled. After going by rope tackle down the slopes, the creek at the bottom was found deep-covered by snow, and travel was possible only after the packhorses went first, breaking a double-track trail for the wagon wheels. And at last, when it seemed that the gulch would go twisting on and on to the limits of the universe, they rolled out in bright winter sunshine with a view of descending benches, foothills, and prairie. And Reverend Klinkke, with his telescope, spotted the rectangles and haystacks of Fort T. M. Hunter, an estimated fifteen miles away.

Old differences were suddenly forgotten. Even Bowers waited his turn at the glass and beat Klinkke on the back in joy. Men who had been lying like corpses on the floor of wagons suddenly got up to see. Food appeared from hiding and was shared. Even the animals seemed to be caught up in the excitement and pulled willingly, helped by the downgrade and the thinning snow, by the hard prairie, and by grass which grew in little pennants to be gobbled in passing.

They came to an ice-covered creek running northwest. There was a bridge, the first such improvement since the Sweetwater back in middle Wyoming. Not a track or a wheel disturbed the snow, but the bridge was there, and a *USA* had been burned into its queen truss for all to see.

"Hip-hip-hooray!" Aldo Rimmel shouted, pointing to the brand.

"Hip-hip-hooray, for the U.S.A." Bowers answered.

"It's sawed timber!" they yelled in joy to the men farther back, trying to whip their teams to a run.

"They got a *sawmill*! We're coming to civilization for sure!"

The bridge had been built to carry wagons laden with sawlogs, some of which had been dumped nearby. Beyond was a hay camp with corrals and the abandoned rectangular cribbing for army tents. The rag remnant of a blue shirt was hung on a gatepost. Horsehair was caught in slivers of the corrals. The shrunken remnants of a haystack attracted the horses, who ate ravenously, grabbing up mouthfuls of hay and snow, and taking the food despite the bits and bridles.

"No moldy hay for mine!" Kavanaugh was whooping. "I'm feeding my teams on bluejoint hay at the Army corrals!"

The valley was half a mile wide and so smooth a wagon could be driven anywhere. The drivers spread out and there was competition for next view of the fort. Cottonwoods had been cleared of underbrush so the wagons took half a dozen routes through the trees. Men fired their guns in the air and looked for the responding cannon puff from the stockade. There was nothing. The stockade stood blank of movement with an unblemished strip of snow clinging to its topmost points. Now it could be seen that all the roofs were gone, and what from far off looked like the snowless roofs of buildings, were actually their blackened insides. A main road, ditched on both sides, ran straight out from the open gates bearing no mark of vehicle, only repeated horse crossings in the older snow. Fort T. M. Hunter had been abandoned.

CHAPTER 5

THE LEAD OUTFITS SLOWED. THEY FINALLY STOPPED altogether and the drivers sat in silence. Back half a mile the revelry of shouting voices sounded like the yapping of coyotes. Garside rode up. He was perfectly leather-faced. He rode in and the wagons followed him.

The great double gate, made to stop charging horses, was unhinged on the ground. What had seemed from great distance to be a flag was actually the shrunken body of a dog which had been run aloft by some joker, Indian or white, and the halyards cut. Gutted and defleshed by magpies, the dog was only strips of skin and hair, and legbones which rattled as the wind swung them back and forth across the pole. Strewn across the yard were some cabinets from which all the hardware had been stripped. The hinges had been taken from the doors, and even the larger spikes had been beaten from the charcoal by Indians who wanted the material for arrowheads. There had obviously been a great traffic of horsemen around and back and forth, and there were signs of open cookfires, but all was now smoothed by the last snow.

One after another the wagons and the packstrings went inside. There were some fresh moccasin tracks. They were all of a certain size, left by one man, and led across the old parade ground. Every building had been burned out, but none of them bore scars of a battle.

Garside waited for all the wagons and spoke: "Well, this is a pretty disappointing reception, but we can thank God we weren't caught when the Indians attacked."

"They never attacked," said Aldo Rimmel. "This fort was abandoned."

"Is it your intention to discredit me?"

"No, I . . ."

"This place obviously suffered an attack in great force. Now, all we can do is hold out here until supplies can be brought from the settlements. Our stock is in no condition to go on. However, there's some hay in the stacks that wouldn't burn; we can remake the shelters and put up the gate. Tomorrow the hunters will go out for game." His eyes rested on Ignatius Denker. It undoubtedly occurred to him that Ignatius and his father must have known of the fort and said nothing. "Now, everyone fall to and make the best of it."

"Why'd he unload on me?" asked Aldo when they went looking at the charred-out haystacks. "Anybody could tell the Army moved out—there wasn't a fight."

"That's the point," said Kavanaugh. "He's been making out that his road will have protection top and bottom from the U.S. Army. This fort was to protect his north flank from the Cheyennes. If they abandon it they'll abandon North Fork, too, and out goes his road scheme like slop from a bucket."

A fight developed at the charred haystacks where the Gileadeans rushed in, taking the best of it in large, loose bales. Dennis and Elwell, piloting the commissary wagon, drove in to break it up and take charge of the distribution, doling the hay a tromped bagful for each animal. Some turnips turned up in a caved root-cellar. They were distributed, and several stews were soon going, meatless but full of fibrous roots. While chopping holes in the creek to water the stock, Everett spied an Indian crouched in the snow and brought him over to Kavanaugh's at rifle point. He was a skeleton in rags—alternately jibbering in fright or laughing—a scavenger, or "digger," and demented.

Denker who had just come in from the hills identified him as a River Crow, and quickly interpreted from his ravings a tale of siege and retreat of the Army which substantiated Garside's appraisal. But afterward Ignatius seated himself on the ground, cross-legged facing the man, and patiently exchanged sign language with him, getting the tale point by point. The fort had been abandoned by the soldiers in late chokecherry-time. They had departed with long freight transports far to the northeastward where the great boat-blowing-fire waited for them. Apparently the Army had maneuvered a steamboat up the Yellowstone during the autumn rise. As soon as they were gone the Cheyennes had burned the fort. Other white men in the area—he gestured to the north, east, and northwest—had departed, and the Indians, many tribes and war parties, had burned their homes, too.

"We should have expected it," said McCoy. "Every time the papers came in from Salt Lake they were filled with senators howling the cost of keeping these northern roads open. And the slaughter at Fort Fetterman. They been moving high heaven to make a deal with the Sioux so the U.P. would have clear sailing across south Wyoming. What they did was trade the U.P. route for all of the country between the Platte and the Yellowstone, and it may not stop there if the truth be known. And woe betide all the settlers depending on this fort."

"Woe betide us, because if the settlers are gone from north of here, where do we find help short of Yellowstone city?"

Crews started tearing down the gutted buildings for logs, and shoveling debris from the buried floors.

McCoy, who never cared for such work, was glad to leave with a hunting party.

It was not a cold day, but an ominous lead blue hung on the horizon. There were eight in the party, and they separated in twos, agreeing to rendezvous at a certain spot which could be seen among the blue-forested foothills to the southwest. With McCoy went the lanky Fisher boy—only seventeen but a good shot. The sun shone dazzling. They wore hoods of old sacking with eye slits to protect them from snow blindness. There were many old tracks in the coulees, but the fresh tracks were only wolves, rabbits and coyotes.

The coyotes were in scattered bands. You saw one, then almost immediately you saw another, and a third, and so on until the total mounted to seven or eight—but never two in the same glance. In the afternoon, after a cold and hungry time, they came to a coulee with thickets, and saw the tracks of a grizzly.

"Isn't it late for these critters?" asked young Fisher.

"When they're out late it's supposed to be sign of a hard winter."

"I'd think it would be the other way around."

"No, they feed as long as they can for a bad one. This fellow might have a berry patch where he could still eat. The chokecherries sometimes freeze and hang by the tons, all gummy with sugar, and a bear chews them like raisins until they're gone. He'll develop fat an inch or two thick, and the most beautiful glossy pelt you ever saw. If you want a good bear-robe, that's the time to shoot it. Of course, if we get this one, our people are so hungry they'll eat it hair and all."

The grizzly's tracks were broad as two outspread palms, and his belly-hair had dragged in the snow. He had followed the coulee in a series of diversions—

swinging in repeatedly as if to climb the bank at its steepest point, going as high as his traction would let him, leaving a gully in the snow where he slid back down.

"He probably just itches on the belly, and the snow feels good to him," said McCoy. "He ploughs up as much snow as that bridle-cow of the Gileadeans, and he wouldn't be half as tough. It wouldn't be bad to have bear meat. We could camp and have the liver now. All the mountain men eat raw liver. But don't overeat. Did you know that a bear's liver is so rich, this time a year, that it'll gorge you sick?"

"I didn't know that."

"And the further north you are, the sicker you'll get."

After a few miles the coulee steepened, and its sides were sprinkled with pine. The horizontal rimrocks, which had resulted in a widened U-bottom, gave place to some lumpy cliffs that looked like rusty lava. With the change of rock, the character of the plants changed. Although it was still sage, buckbrush and pine, all grew thicker and higher, and with darker, more lustrous bark. And the grass was so deep and snow-clotted it became an impediment to travel.

They grazed their hungry horses for a while, and resumed traveling, following the bear tracks over a milewide hump of the hills and down into another coulee. There the tracks turned back toward the north, climbing repeatedly to the coulee crest which offered a view of the country.

"He must have been watching *us*," said young Fisher.

"No, he couldn't have seen us. Maybe he was watching Jake and Ellis."

"Or Indians."

"There's no Indian sign. They're all up along the

Yellowstone, hunting down the poor-devil settlers—all those homesteaders under The Act, come to farm beneath the protecting guns of Fort Hunter, and now abandoned by their government. They ought to form an army, commandeer a train on that precious railroad, and camp on the grass of the White House."

"You really think so?" asked young Fisher, open-mouthed.

"No, not actually. When you start digging into right and wrong you'll end up with an awful deep well. The government gave 'em the land but if you were a Cheyenne you'd say it wasn't theirs to give. On the other hand, how'd the Cheyennes come by it? Well, I'll tell you—they shot off the Shoshones."

The boy stared at him. He seemed awed. It made McCoy feel like one old in wisdom. He smiled, and his face, set by the cold, hurt where the bones had been broken. He wondered how he looked. There was a mirror at the Hulbush wagon—he would call and use it. Perhaps I will look cynical and worldly, he thought, with my broken face. Or more likely, like some scheming trader in the newspaper cartoons.

"Everybody sees right and wrong from his own point of view," he said.

"Even sons-of-bitches like Garside?"

"Yes, even sons-of-bitches like Garside. He cares no more for a man than he does for a dog. Less, because he might sell a dog. But what would have happened if a nice fellow like Aldo was captain? The Gileadeans would have gone one way and us the other, both cut up by Indians. We're ragged and bobtailed, but we're alive. We're hunting and other people are building and there'll be warm fires when we get back."

"Is that why you never fought him?"

145

"Maybe I never fought Garside because I didn't feel I could win."

"You'd win, all right. Doc tells how you can handle a gun. And your fists, too."

"He's bigger than I am."

"Not much."

McCoy never felt he could lick Garside, but it had nothing to do with physical prowess. He would not win because he did not have to win. He was not impelled by Garside's crushing, driving necessity. He did not have the will, put it that way. He never felt there was anything so important that he had to fight for it until he was dead. But Garside did. When Garside got a bloodshot eye on something there was nothing could stop him.

"Son, I'll tell you," he said, "I've noticed that the Garsides of this world always win and the McCoys always lose. That is, in the pure realm of the physical— property, bank accounts, et cetera. Not in the realm of personal satisfaction—but maybe *that's* just a point of view."

An odor of woodsmoke guided them to the rendezvous—and as they grew close, the broiling of meat. One of the parties had come in with five sage hens, birds the size of small turkeys with tough bluish breast-meat. The men ate and slept ringed by small campfires, taking turns getting up to tend them. Next morning they breakfasted on the remnants of sage hen and sugar biscuits Elwell had stolen from Tunis' supply. McCoy and Fisher went back for their bear and the others split in twos to comb the upcountry for deer. It started to storm, and the bear trail filled with blown snow. The snow came very heavy, but so warm that it stuck wet and made a trickle down the horses' coats.

146

Then the wind swung to the north, and the temperature dropped. At a coulee-turning the wind caught them full, with a piercing blast which made the horses balk, and no amount of urging could keep them from swinging about with their tails to it.

They retreated and found a hollowed bank with dirt and washed-out roots above, and a deep pad of leaves and dead brush under the snow. It was too windy for a fire. Somehow, stamping and walking, dozing for quarter-hours and walking again, they managed to keep from freezing, and the day passed, and the long darkness; next morning, in a quiet of the storm, they reached the fort.

The hunters came in until all were accounted for. Two of them arrived with the carcass of a small deer, the prize take, but it vanished half-a-pound to the ration in a single day. The hunters became used to spending most of their time in the open, returning every second or third day, spending a night under roof, and going out again. One group came in dragging five elk, having found a herd moving toward the Big Horn; but more often the bag was light, consisting of rabbits, a few sage hens, even a wolf or coyote—for as the blue hunger settled, no meat was ignored.

Whatever came in was strictly rationed. The meat was weighed on an improvised beam and put away in the cache house, a solid little building on high piles, and guarded day and night by one or another of the Major's men. Somehow, good hunting or poor, there were always rations for four or five more days.

Other buildings had risen, mostly on the old foundations. The logs were reused, their charred sides outward and caulked with mud which froze hard as iron.

Roofs were of poles and dirt, or canvas over poles, and the ice which formed was a sealer. There was fuel in plenty in the old wood-lot—green wood but willing to burn hissing-hot in an already hot fire—and many of the wagons had carried sheetmetal stoves. More permanent heating arrangements were fashioned of bricks, clay, and old iron plates. It was always blistering hot near the stoves and cold near the walls, so a person could turn his hindside and see his breath at the same time; and as the days went by frost gathered on the logs, turning the insides of the houses into crystal caves.

The largest of the structures, built highest of the best logs, served Garside as his headquarters; there he spent most of his time, alone or with his loyal Abel Tunis, pacing or sitting or standing hours at his window of pieced-together glass, looking out at the yard, and the white desolation.

The storm continued. There were lulls of a day or so, and then it would come on again, always from the same direction—slightly north of east—across the level ground that apparently stretched away to the Great Barrens. Snow piled up until in places one could climb on wind-packed crust to the edges of roofs, and Garside had his men out shoveling an unobstructed view of the gate so he could watch everyone who came and went.

He was standing by his window late one afternoon and saw Brother Thomas outside speaking to Tunis. In a minute Tunis came inside.

"Elder Hulbush wants to see you."

"Is it important?" he asked without moving.

"I guess it is."

"Did he say the Elder was worse?"

"He doin' poorly."

If the Elder died, which seemed probable, Garside

knew what difficulty he would have in controlling these people who were so important to his enterprise.

"Tell him I'll come directly."

When Abel returned Garside asked to have fresh clothing laid out and water heated on the brick and metal stove. He sat down to be shaved; someone rapped, and he cursed silently when Abel told him it was Pet.

"She say her papa send her," said Abel.

She had been living with her father, Ignatius, and a French quarter-breed hunter named Laroque, at some old freighter's quarters which had been dug into the side of a bank about a mile down the coulee.

"All right, let her in."

Now that she stood before him he had a quick desire for her. She showed no pregnancy in the blanket-gown and he knew by experience how marvelously simple it would be to slide the loose coverings upward from her strong young body, but the Negro stood watching, and to send him outside would be to invite notice from the Gileadeans.

She handed him something wrapped in a burlap sack. He looked and saw five trout, all of a size-about twelve inches. They were silvery fish with large spots which grew more numerous at the tails, and with scarlet gashes of color under throats. They looked almost alive under their glass-clear coatings of ice.

"Papa send."

The food situation evidently was very good if Denker was willing to share.

"Tell him many thanks."

"All right. I go now?"

She was ready to lie down for him, but Garside, despite his need, said, "Yes"—making one more sacrifice for the road, for his future, for appearances before the watching Gileadeans.

"Goodbye," said Pet.

He wanted to say, "Wait, I'll see you tonight," but it was too risky, so he said, "Goodbye," and allowed her to leave.

He bathed and let Tunis finish shaving him. While dressing he had Tunis fry the trout, using some precious lard. Odor of the fish, so golden-greasy after turnip and horse meat, proved too much for him, and he ate one hot from the pan. Leaving one for Tunis, he took the other three, paper-wrapped, for a gift to Hulbush.

An early twilight was settling. It was very cold. The smoke seemed to congeal over a dozen stovepipes. He could hear the runners of the wood sled a quarter-mile away. His boots made creaking sounds as he walked in the packed snow. He guessed the temperature at thirty below zero.

The Gileadeans had taken over one whole side of the cantonment, and had built, using the stockade for a continuous rear wall, a long, narrow shed which served communally for people and animals. Several partly-burned buildings which stood in the course of the shed had also been rebuilt after a manner, and the old harness rooms became a temple; the shacks of some civilian employees were now homes for Reverend Klinkke and other leaders; and a squarish building, probably the home of the master saddler or another civilian employee, had been taken over by Elder Hulbush.

Bethel herself came to the door of the shed which served as a storm entrance to the house. She spoke, and though he could barely see her, still was instantly and forcibly aware of how she looked, and everything about her. She was almost of a size with Pet—strong and ample in the thighs and abdomen—and he wanted her suddenly in a way which made his desire for Pet only a spiritless substitute.

"Bethel!" he said, reaching for at least the comfort of her hand, he needed her so; but she moved back in the steamy darkness—pungent from mules, urine, and hay—just beyond him.

"How is he?"

"Papa isn't well. If only it would get warm for a day or two!"

"Yes, it's been very trying, my dear."

The door was covered by canvas to stop the draft, and they went inside a small room curtained down the middle by more canvas and an old blanket or two. He knew by the sound of breathing that Hulbush lay beyond. A candle about one inch long was burning.

"What's this?" she asked, catching her breath at the aroma of oily fried trout.

"I had these caught especially for him. We must give him strength. What would we do without his spiritual guidance?"

"I'll see if he can eat one. Part of one, anyway."

"And we'll have the others."

"No, I must share."

But she was very hungry, and he noticed how her eyes shone in the candlelight as she looked at the fish with their greasy, crackly coatings.

"This once, my dear."

"All right, but after Papa."

She took the candle and carried it around the curtain where Hulbush lay in a pole-and-slat bed. He was emaciated, but his eyes were alive, shifting and feverishly bright in the midst of his dead man's face. He smelled the trout and sat up with a sudden jerk as if on springs. He seemed ravenous, but after a couple of mouthfuls his appetite and strength failed suddenly and he fell back and started to cough. He coughed and coughed until it seemed that coughing would be the end of him, but finally, with a shudder and a long wheeze, he recovered and lay weak but comprehending.

"Bless you, Brother. May God bless you. You are a noble man. We would be dead and scattered to the winds without you, Brother Garside."

Garside stood with head bowed in acceptance of the tribute.

"I am soon to die, Brother. I will not see this coldness out."

"No, Brother Hulbush, this will not be."

"Please, it is true. This cold, it settles in my bones and no warmth of fire drives it out again."

"Brother Hulbush . . ."

Hulbush stopped him with his bloodless fingers. "Hear me, I will die this winter. From this coldness I pass over into Jordan. I want only one thing. You, my son, and you, my daughter." He called them to him and put her hand in Garside's. "Bethel, my daughter. And you, Henry, my son. I may call you Henry?"

"You may call me Henry and son. From your lips . . ." He seemed quite overcome. "From your lips they are the dearest words I have ever heard."

"I pray for one thing yet in this land of living, and it is that you two be wed. I had two sons. Both, both abandoned me. But now, at last, I have wish to feel that there would be other sons—my grandsons who are yet to be, the issue of your holy union."

"Papa," Bethel said, "After a while. You're . . ."

"No, we have waited far too long. I am not going to get well. The wedding must be now. Now, before this cold creeps into me deeper."

Garside looked at Bethel and for an instant she met his eyes. He tried to show her how much he cared for her, the very particular nature of his feeling, and he held out his hand. After a second she placed her hand in his. He held her strongly to show how he loved her, desired her, wished with all his heart and body to make the old man's wish come true—make her fruitful and bring sons and daughters into the new land.

Hulbush seemed deeply gratified. "I will die in peace. You have made me happy. Will you call Brother Klinkke."

"When?" asked Bethel, sounding frightened.

"Now, this evening."

"Oh, no, we can't. You don't understand . . ."

"I understand that there are many times when I feel hanging between life and death. But with you married, and this man to go on leading our people, then with what peace I would go to my Father's bosom!"

"But there are so many things to do!" said Bethel.

"Tomorrow, perhaps?" said Garside, seeking her trust.

"Very well then," said Hulbush. "Tomorrow."

At noon McCoy, Ignatius, young Fisher, and Elwell came in carrying a quartered-out deer. They were on foot, carrying snowshoes which were of little use when one left the deep snow of the foothills. Tunis saw them and came to the cache house to weigh the meat and jot it in his records, and Garside followed him, strangely nervous, a barely-controlled elation in every movement.

"What's got into *him*?" McCoy asked when he left.

Tunis said, "Why, I suppose Mist' Major feels right happy about you bringing in a nice, fat venison for his marriage feast. It's like Providence he get it today. Just like Providence."

He spoke with relish, enjoying the chance of turning the blade in McCoy, a man he had never liked much.

"You mean Garside is finally going to marry that poor Indian girl he got with child?" he asked, seeing Ignatius was out of earshot.

"I shorely don't know what you talking about."

"I think you *shorely* do."

"No, sir! And I'm going to pretend like I never heard you say that. I wouldn't want to pass a tale like that around. It could get a man in trouble. I'm talkin' about his marriage with Miss Bethel Hulbush."

"When?"

"To-o-o-night!" he said, drawing it out smacking-good on his tongue. "Oh, it'll be something. It really will. How they been stirring around! Goodness gracious, you never seen such a getting-out of clothes, and patching, and pressing, and cooking. You wouldn't believe the honey and raisins and such they managed to have tucked away. Only thing they didn't have was some nice, tender venison with the fat on it. This fat lardin' around the inside is sho'ly going to come in handy to make a wedding pie, and cookie-cakes, and maybe a fig pudding."

McCoy looked at him tough-faced. "They can use their half for anything they want, Tunis."

"Their *three-fifths,* you mean. Or half plus giblets."

It had become the custom to give the Gileadeans sixty pounds in every hundred of the meat which came in, but as it was difficult to divide a carcass in that proportion, Garside had ordered them to be quartered or sided out as usual, the extra ten percent being made up of heart, liver, tongue, kidneys and such smaller parts.

"By the way," said Abel, "where are those giblets? All I find here is lungs and one end of tongue meat."

They had eaten tongue, heart, liver, and brains in camp the night before, and the sweetbreads, roasted in the ashes, were cracked like nuts and chewed the next morning.

"They no giblets here."

"Half and half, Tunis. It's not my fault we shot a deer that didn't have giblets."

"Mist' Major ain't going to like that."

"Hunter's privilege!"

"A rule's a rule, that's how we all stay alive."

"You stay alive real well, Abel. Even if the Major would suddenly not be around I'd bet you'd stay alive."

"Well, ha-ha. I'd try."

"That's what I like about you, Abel. You stay nice and sleek. I'd say, barring the chance of an accident, you're almost sure to be one of the survivors."

"Yes. Well, I won't make mention about the giblets and maybe Mist' Major will forget 'em this once. Or I'll say I made it up with lard, seeing it's what they needed. He ain't likely to take too much notice. He's being anointed by the Gileadeans."

"He's what?"

"Being anointed. You wash all over and they rub you with herbs and perfume and stuff. It all comes out of the Good Book. And you know what part of him they anoint the very most? You know what that part is, Mist' McCoy?"

McCoy ignored him, but it was an effort. He called Chuck Rimmel inside to supervise the division of meat saying, "I got to get to the house. I'm falling-down tired."

He was indeed tired. He had been on the hunt for three days. They had bagged the deer yesterday, and decided to take a shortcut to the fort, crossing the grain

155

of the country from gulch to gulch which entailed steep climbing, and night caught them. That was when the giblets were eaten, washed down with an "Indian tea" made by Ignatius of snow water and certain twigs— bitter draught that left everyone feeling slightly drunk, and as if he were twelve feet tall. A man needed more than tea before morning came, with the temperature down to an estimated thirty below. You slept in five-and ten-minute snatches and woke up to stamp life into your body and hunt more frozen wood for the fires.

He did not immediately seek rest, however. Leaving Chuck to watch the division of venison he went to the Gileadean quarters. He started to rap, but he was being watched; the door opened, and a woman stood facing him. She was a solid, undersized woman with a red face and small eyes.

"What do you want?" she asked.

"I came to see Bethel Hulbush."

"Not here!" and she started to close the door. It was a heavy door which scraped and had to be levered shut with a full thrust of the shoulder, and McCoy stopped her.

"Not here!" she repeated. "Get out of the door."

She kept ramming the door against his knee, but he did not retreat. He was sick of these people, of whom the woman was a good example: crude and morose, ignorantly huddling against the world as God's chosen ones. He pushed the door open and walked past. It was dark in the long tunnel structure which smelled of dung. People were living in the same room with mules. They still had some chickens—brought over the pass in great awkward crates on the backs of mules—and he could hear their cackling. Despite the odors, the ground everywhere was clean as earth could be made.

156

The woman followed him, talking furiously and trying to grab him, but he walked straight on. Others came, shawl-wrapped women and bearded men. The men always wore their funny round hats in the house. Outside they wrapped shawls over their heads and set their round hats on top. He had grown to hate the sight of those round, black hats.

The men stopped him. Reverend Klinkke arrived.

"He asks for Sister Hulbush," a Gileadean said to Klinkke.

"So what of that?"

Klinkke was tall, he had skinny legs, and his boots seemed preposterous in size. McCoy had heard Klinkke preach. It was Hell's fire even at funerals with the saddened relatives standing by. His protruding eyes and forked beard gave him an Old Testament look of prophets gone mad. Klinkke did not doubt that all humans had been born in sin and were evil to the end of their days. He believed the worst of everyone. Hence he believed the worst of Garside.

"You come to see Sister Hulbush?" he asked. "Come with me." He called, "Sister Hulbush!" at a canvas door. "The renegade from Montana would speak with thee."

They entered a small, square house half curtained off, dim with parchment-covered windows, air smelling strongly of camphor. He heard the steps of Bethel without being able to see her. Old Hulbush was coughing. He coughed steadily and quietly, as if it had become a necessary part of breathing. Klinkke remained in the door. "Thanks," said McCoy, and closed him outside. Then he turned, realizing that Bethel was before him.

"I don't want to see you!" she said.

"But you are seeing me."

"Go away!" she whispered. She was frightened. He thought, not of me, then what is she frightened of? Was she afraid he might change her mind about marrying Garside?

"No, I'm not going away. Not until you listen to me. You can't marry that man. Do you realize he has that poor half-breed girl with child?"

"She is Halleck's wife."

"Were you at the marriage?"

"But they were married according to the Indian custom."

"Where is he now?"

"I don't know. He ran away. . . or, maybe the Indians . . . I . . ."

"Why did he beat her?"

"It's not my affair. It was only gossip."

"He beat her when he found out she was getting big with child about ten days after their so-called marriage. He beat her and she ran to Kavanaugh's wagon for protection. Then Garside came and took her away, and nobody has seen Halleck since."

She refused to hear him, but he walked and cornered her against a wall.

"Have you asked yourself what happened to Halleck when he faced Garside about the baby? He disappeared without a horse being gone. One of Garside's own men told me that."

"They all hate him. He's saved us from going off in ten directions under your leadership, or under Kavanaugh's. Yes, even under Klinkke, and Brother Siles who would have taken off for the gold fields! But he saved us, and everyone hates him for it."

"What about the Denker girl? Will you come with me?"

158

"Where?" she asked, alarmed.

"To see her."

"It wouldn't prove anything."

The coughing had stopped. They listened to the complete quiet beyond the curtain.

"Come here," said Elder Hulbush in a dry, wheezy voice. She did, and he said, "Both, both."

McCoy stood and looked down on him.

"Why do you come to disquiet us?" asked Hulbush. "You are not of us, and desire not to be of us. Still, we have done you no evil, only kindness, taking you in—a stranger and wounded."

"That is true. But I care for your daughter greatly. What order of man would I be to hide and be silent while she married a man who has been the undoing of one girl, abandoning her with child?"

"How can you say this is his child?"

"I do say it."

"Aye. I believe you."

"You *believe me*? Then, good God . . ."

"Yes, God is good unto the righteous who keep His laws, but the laws of God are different unto great men and small. When Rehoboam came to Jerusalem, he who was the son of Solomon, was he not warlike and intent to set himself up to fight his brethren, the people of Judah and Benjamin? And did not the Lord God Jehovah, although knowing Rehoboam was a man of blood and of war and withal a tyrant, say to his chosen people, 'Return, for this which does Rehoboam is done of me.' And did not then Rehoboam, being a great leader although a man of lust and of blood, do great things building cities? Did he not build Bethlehem, Etam and Tekoa? And also Beth-aur and Gath and Azekah made he them. And in

159

every city, being warlike, did he place shields and spears making them strong having Jehovah on his side, and also ordained he priests for high places and for devils. Then Rehoboam took him Mahalath the daughter of Jerimoth; and also took he Abigail, which bare him children; and he took Maachah the daughter of Absalom which bare him children; in all, eighteen wives and concubines to his bed for his need was strong, and in all his was he blessed of the Lord. For weak men with no need of women are not those who raise great cities with gates of brass. Only when Rehoboam defied him the laws of God was he struck down and made humble. And only when making himself humble was he lifted up again. So I say to you, McCoy, stand not in among us to turn our women from the ways of strength. I tell you that this man was sent us by God for the regeneration of our people, and to raise cities on these plains. So go, and do not trouble us."

He turned on Bethel, "What do *you* think of this?"

She shook her head and gestured that he should go.

"No, I'm not leaving without an answer. Are you willing to be one of the many women of this modern-day Rehoboam?"

"Go away. Can't you leave us be?"

"Then you think it's all right for him to leave that poor half-breed girl . . ."

"Please. Please go."

He saw it was useless. He left her. The Gileadeans watched him in their bovine impassiveness as he walked away.

"I'm going hunting again," he said to Chuck Rimmel.

"But good God . . ."

"There's some buffalo wintering down from the hills, fifteen or twenty, and I think I know where to find them."

"You going *alone*?"

"Beauchamp and his bunch are in the area—I'll swing up north and camp at their meeting place. I'll be all right."

"Say, you're gone on that Gileadean girl, aren't you?"

"I don't know whether it's that, or whether I just so hate the yellow guts of Garside."

The Temple had once been used to store cavalry equipment, and the civilian saddle-maker had had his bench behind a railing in the back. Everything had been taken away when the Army left except some rude tables and the puncheon horses where the saddles rested while waiting their turn to be repaired. The building had had a square, pyramidal roof with a chimney in the center; Indians, coming soon after the Army's departure, had set it afire by means of faggots tossed to the roof, and it had burned downward, collapsing and charring through the floor, but the walls, of mill-squared cottonwood with the sap still in, smoldered and went out, leaving them blackened but with solid heartwood.

The Gileadeans had rebuilt the room, scraping the char from the logs leaving them a rich brown, and rebuilding the old, fallen chimney to form a central pillar for the roof. Benches had been built all around the wall, and a rough pulpit in the middle. The only window opening, of parchment, had proved cold and ineffective and had been covered with pieces of plank. On bright days a glow came through the roof, which was of poles and canvas, covered by snow. On meeting days, and nights—for the Gileadeans spent much time at sermon, testimony, and prayer—a pitch lamp was lit.

161

That night, four pitch lamps were burning, one at each corner, and there was a large candle in an iron tripod by the pulpit. Smoke rose in sooty ribbons over the pitch flames, but after the darkness of other rooms it seemed brilliant. A tiny organ had been brought over the mountains despite all difficulties, and a large, horse-faced girl sat at it playing hymns.

The people came and sat, men on two sides of the room, and their women across from them. All were washed, patched, and polished. The women sat with their long skirts drawn around their shoes, and their feet together. The men were allowed greater laxity, and they chewed and spit on the ground. They did not spit in front of them, however. They sat and chewed, and tilted their heads to one side and let the brown tobacco-liquor fall politely from the sides of their lips, and afterward they would wipe their beards, passing their open hands downward. And they would clear their throats, shift to new positions, and scratch.

After what seemed to be a very long wait, Reverend Klinkke entered, dressed in his black suit and freshly tallowed boots, and commenced to preach. After an extended sermon, he cleared his throat and announced that they were met to join Sister Hulbush and Brother Garside in wedlock, and the wedding party entered.

Brother Zuph and some of the other leading Gileadeans came first, then—and there was a mutter of excitement from the congregation—Elder Hulbush, dressed but spectral thin, on the arm of Elder Englehardt. Bethel Hulbush and Garside came next— Bethel garbed in a long, simple garment of light gray, with a hood fastened at her chin and falling to her waist, and Garside erect with every button and buckle polished to a military brilliance.

"We are come now to join this man and this woman in the bonds of holy wedlock," Reverend Klinkke said. He turned and called, "What is thy name, sister?"

"Bethel Hulbush," she answered almost inaudibly. Then she stood straighter and said, "Bethel Hulbush!"

"And thy name, brother?"

"I am Henry Baugh Garside."

"Who is this man with thee?"

"I am Isaac Hulbush."

"Are you the woman's father?"

"I am."

"Is it thy will she be wed to this man, Henry Baugh Garside?"

"It is."

"Then let this man and this woman join hands and, come before me to be wed in the sight of God."

However, as they started around the pulpit, and to the right of the candle, there was a commotion outside. Klinkke leafed through his Bible for a time waiting for it to cease, but it did not. There seemed to be a fight in progress. Several men were shouting. There was cursing, and what sounded like a strangled cry for help.

Klinkke said, "Brother Rolf, will you see what's the tantrum-trouble out there? Mayhap Brother John needs some help."

Brother John was the head sentry, and the only Gileadean who customarily went armed with a pistol.

Brother Rolf, followed by others, pulled the door open letting in a blast of cold which whipped the lights. There was a tussle between John and a man who proved to be Aldo Rimmel. It was big Aldo who had been doing the cursing, and he was cursing bitterly now. There were more men in the darkness, and the Gileadeans were up to meet what was evidently an onslaught.

163

"We don't want any trouble," a voice recognizable as Kavanaugh's said. "We're just here to see that this kid gets a fair and square hearing."

"What is it troubling thee?" demanded Klinkke. "This is a house of worship."

"Let the kid have his say!"

It was Ignatius Denker.

"No!" cried Garside. "You! Denker, go back to your camp! I'll come over and talk to you."

"You'll talk to me here!" cried Ignatius. Lithe as a bobcat, he twisted and got inside. He made it, and backed along the wall, ready for attack. His hand rested on a hunting knife in the sash at his waist. His eyes darted in every direction, but he never completely stopped looking at Garside. Outside, the struggle had stopped and men picked themselves up from the snow. Gileadeans and Gentiles watched the slim half-breed boy to see what he would do.

"Why do you come here to this holy place?" asked Klinkke. "Why do you trouble us?"

"He is the husband of my sister," Ignatious answered, pointing to Garside. "Yes, you are husband of my sister."

Garside motioned for quiet and spoke to him and to everybody. "No, I am not husband of your sister. My cousin was her husband, and if it be true that he has deserted her, then I will assume the responsibility of her support. Ignatius, I told your father that. He was satisfied. She knows that. Now, go back and talk to them. And take these people . . ."

"You are father of her baby!"

It had created a stir among the Gileadeans, and more and more people crowded from outside to watch. The room rapidly chilled, and draught whipped the lamp flames.

164

Garside controlled his temper and spoke in a clear, biting voice. "No, I am *not* the father of her baby." He turned and said, "Before God I am not! I fully realize the stories that have been passed around. Believe them if you wish. There are always some who will believe. But those of you who are fair of mind will hear me when I say they are carried by those who want to destroy me, undercut my authority, cause you to lose faith in me, cast me out. I tell you a lie like that is aimed at all of us!" He must have sensed doubt in the heavy Gileadean faces turned toward him, for he lifted both hands, looked at Hulbush and Bethel, at Klinkke, and slowly at the others, and spoke clearly: "Before God, the Almighty, I swear that I am not the father of this poor girl's child, if child she has. I count three, and O Almighty God, may I be struck dead by Thy lightenings if what this boy says is true." And in the awed hush he counted, "One! Two!" and, "Three!"

At the count of three a mass exhalation could be heard. And they believed him. Garside knew they believed him, and he stood with his head high, and he smiled in an almost beatified manner, knowing they believed.

"She has your baby!" cried Ignatius. "You son-of-a-bitch! Every night you would come to be in bed with her. I saw you leaving her bed."

"Take him out of here!" Garside said, turning to Brother John.

John attempted to seize him, but the young half-breed was too quick. He dodged under, leaving John empty-armed, facing in the wrong direction. John turned and collided with one of his bearded brethren. The knife shone in Ignatius' hand. It made a butcher's gleam, more deadly seeming than any gun, and a terror, half

165

revulsion, passed through the room. Men and women tried to get out of the way. With a thud, something of wood went over. Boots were an audible scraping on the dirt floor. The room was only half-light. A pitch lamp had been rammed to one side.

Garside's voice: "Don't move, anyone."

They turned and saw him holding a small pistol. His command which stopped them had left Ignatius revealed. Briefly he was in the open and no one behind in the line of fire, and Garside pulled the trigger. The gun flashed, and its bullet made a distinct thud, like a hammer hitting beef. Ignatius had been weaving forward with his knife almost touching the floor, and as the gun flashed he was coming forward to swing the blade upward toward Garside's groin. The impact, at a range of no more than ten feet, diverted his rush; it spun him like a dancer on one moccasined foot. He lashed with the knife and fell. He kept trying to get up but the weight of the wound seemed to pull him down again, and he swung the knife in a futile, horizontal savagery, the blind anger of a wounded rattlesnake.

The gunshot had started a rush for the doors. A pitch light overturning, spraying flammable half-liquid gum, spread fire across one wall. People were down and trampled on. The room was ruddy and filled with a peculiar light. The fire seemed to go out, then it burst out, driving away the few who seized robes and hats and tried to fight it. The packed humanity proved too much for one of the crib-log walls which spilled outward. People ran through the snow filling their lungs with the cold air, and after a while Bethel Hulbush could be heard shouting, "He's in there! Papa is in there!"

Two men held her. She twisted and fought to the ground trying to get loose and return inside the flame-ruddy room.

"They're going in after him," one of the men said. "Brother Samuel is in there now."

It was not Brother Samuel but Aldo Rimmel, and he came out holding the old man as if he were a bag of hay. Blind and wheezing from the smoke, he carried him, and dropped him.

"To hell with that old son-of-a-bitch," Bowers was yelling. "Where's the kid? You going to leave him in there shot?"

"He's out!" said the other Rimmel.

"Well, where is he?"

"Never mind where he is. Do you want Garside to finish him?"

"He'll have to kill me before he finishes him."

The fire mounted and the roof collapsed. Mules were led out and snow was shoveled on the long sheds to confine the fire. The flames climbed like a great torch which lit the hills a mile away, but they did not spread, and in half an hour the old harness-house-turned-temple became a square of coals hissing and sputtering down to its damp sill logs.

McCoy had left the fort about an hour before sundown. On his way out, carrying blankets and snowshoes, his rifle, and a small packet of food, he had met Ignatius Denker. The young half-breed knew he had been at the Gileadeans', and no doubt suspected why.

"*She* is to be his wife?" asked Ignatius.

"Yes." McCoy could then have walked past him through the gate but he obeyed an impulse, almost instantly regretted: "How about your sister?"

"What of my sister?" Ignatius sprang in front of him. "What! what!"

"Oh, hell, you know the answer to that. You know

167

whose baby she's having."

"I will kill him."

"Now, hold on. That's not your job at all. Go to your father. Talk about it to him."

"I have talked to him about it."

"Well, go back and talk to him some more."

He left, not knowing by Ignatius' dark manner whether he would return to his father's camp or not.

Traveling at a distance-hungry stride, an alternate walk and trot, he fastened on the snowshoes at the first coulee and crossed toward the forested hills. Effort and fatigue in the cold air soon glazed his senses. He became a thing of looking, breathing, and walking. He traveled as the sun set in mist, and darkness came. There were some stars through the scattering jackpine trees. He found an old camp—a brush shelter, some buried fuel. He melted some snow and boiled the underbark of cottonwood to make a tea. It was sweet, passing into his veins like alcohol. He felt a drunken, angry energy, and he cursed himself for having run away. But it passed; he ate some fire-dried strips of venison, and fatigue took its place. Fatigue weighted every fiber of his body so he could scarcely summon the movement necessary to dig a bed beneath pine boughs and snow, get in boots-first, and pull the blanket over him. He lay with his eyes open for a while, looking at a thin strip of moon through the openings of twigs and snow. Then he closed his eyes. He had only an hour before the cold would creep in, and he would have to get out and move around, build the fire, heat the sugar-bark tea to a steaming, warm his inside. A few crystals of snow settled. A wolf howled. A twig snapped in the fire . . .

He awoke suddenly, without alarm, but as if someone had called him from a distance. He was chilled and it

168

took a while to move. Arising, he saw the clearing quiet in the moonlight. Snow made it bright as day. He got up. He stamped some warmth into his body and climbed a switchback footpath to a small summit. The fort was visible, and he saw the fire. It was rising to an apex. Burning fragments were carried in the air. There were moving shadows. The entire stockade seemed to be burning out, but later the flames died, and he could see buildings in silhouette. By this he knew the fire must be on the far side, in the Gileadean quarters. It occurred to him that there had been a fight. But there had been no sound of gunfire. Even at eight miles, across the snow, he would have heard any extended rifle fire.

He watched as the flames shrank to a glow. Waking and sleeping he endured the night. By dawn the fort was visible with a blackened spot at one side. A mist of smoke hung in the coulees.

He overcame the impulse to go back. There were some fresh deer-tracks which he followed into the timber. Wind blew deadly cold. He lost the deer in drifting snow. The country was empty. Even the rabbits were gone. He spent a second night, and turned back toward the fort. All seemed to be the same except for the place where the meeting house had burned out, leaving the Gileadean quarters in two segments. Some men in round hats turned to look at him.

"I didn't even shoot my food," he said, falling on a straw pallet in Kavanaugh's smoky quarters.

"Well, you brought in enough betimes, and we have some hind leg of mule, *au jus*. What do you think of that? The Major gave it out to butcher one of the "Hog-all" animals for a change." He added, "Of course, it was burned-limping in the fire."

He told about the fracas, and McCoy waited with

169

stilled breathing to learn that Bethel had not been married after all. It all seemed like an act of providence. But there was poor wounded Ignatius, and McCoy was in a way responsible.

"How is the kid?"

"He's alive. Garside would have killed him that night if he'd found him. He came storming through with that army of his—Dennis and the rest—and the Gileadeans backing 'em, but we kept the kid out of sight. They came right in the room with him, and he was lying over yonder under a robe, not making a sound. A God damn Injun, but you got to give 'em credit . . ."

"Will he make it?"

"I don't have an answer to that. Doc probed for the bullet and got hunks of it. It split on a rib, and I don't know if he got all of it or not. We melted what he had and recast it, and it made just exactly one of those forty-caliber round balls, so we figure we got it all. If we didn't he'll sicken with the green pus in about ten days, and of course it'll be all up with him. But I think it's pretty much in his favor."

"Where is he? At his dad's camp?"

"Yes, down there holed up in one of those dugouts. They're all down there: the Denkers, that breed hunter La Rock, and somebody named Jim Smoke—I suppose he's Injun, too. Garside knows he's there, but he ain't asking for any bullets. Bigfoot was pretty sore. You can understand it, kid shot and girl pregnant both by the same man. It upsets a father, even if the kids are half-Injun."

He ate, forcing himself to go slow on the gruel of mule meat.

"How about Hulbush?"

"They never tell us nothing. I guess he's alive or

170

they'd be funeralizing. Aldo carried him out of the fire. They never even thanked him. Those people are like cattle. If they're God's chosen, then I'll go along with the devil. That's a terrible thing to say, but I would. Oh, some of 'em are all right. Brother Siles I like, but he'd quit and head for Montana if he had the chance. That just shows you."

"Is Bethel over there?"

"She went someplace."

"When?"

"This morning, just sunup."

"Who with?"

It was a relief when Kavanaugh said, "With some woman. They went out to dig medicinal herbs. Going to treat the old man with 'em."

"Dig herbs? The ground is frozen like iron."

"Bark, then. They practice witchcraft. Stuff from the Bible, but it's witchcraft all the same. You should have heard the cure they had for my lumbago. First off I was to purge myself three days and three nights. I'd have died. And when Brother Vande-what's-his-name had the blood poison Klinkke had his arm wrapped up in a live bullsnake."

"He lived."

"Yah, he lived," Kavanaugh said truculently.

He alternately slept and watched for Bethel. When she did not return and the sun was slanting toward the horizon in late afternoon, he went to inquire where she had gone.

"Sister Hulbush is catching birds for the treatment of her father who is very poorly with the lung fever," said Reverend Klinkke.

"Oh, *birds.* I thought she went for herbs."

"Those too, Brother. Major Garside came to douse him with medicines, or sent his black man to do it, but they were without effect. Now we treat him after the manner set forth in the Testament. It is the word of Moses that the priest shall take two birds alive and clean, and cedar wood, and hyssop and scarlet. But not birds which have lived on things unclean; but birds of the forest, other than birds of prey, they are clean. And one of them shall be killed in an earthen dish over running water. The other then to be taken and be dipped in the blood of the killed bird, and the cedar wood, also hyssop and scarlet. And the priest shall sprinkle him who is sick of a pus-forming disease, and pronounce him clean. You see, Brother Hulbush has only since the fire made pus, which is an unclean disease after the meaning of the Testament. But then the living bird will be loosed into a field, and on the seventh day the clothing is to be washed seven times pronouncing him cured of his illness. Also shave off his hair and beard and eyebrows. And wash away his fever-heat with water. Then after the eighth day will we take two lambs without blemish, or other animals without blemish, and flour mingled with oil—the priest to present him who is to be made clean before the Lord, at the door of the tabernacle, and shall slay one lamb, and place some of the blood on the tip of the right ear of the sick man, and on the thumb of his right hand, and the great toe of his right foot, but be shall also swear seven times unto the Lord, it is in the Book of Leviticus, called betimes the Third Book of Moses."

"And that is going to cure him?"

"It is!"

"That is where she went . . . for the clean birds?"

"The birds that picketh seeds from the plants, and not carrion which is unclean. But not sparrows, either. But grouse."

"She has to bring them alive."

"Yes, with the quick blood in them."

"Where did she go?"

"It is not man's province to know."

"You sent her out alone?"

"She went willingly, and not alone. She left with Sister Zellner, wife of Brother Nephi Zellner who knows much of grouse, having come in with many birds from a favored coulee."

"It's pretty cold."

"They know what they do, Brother, and it is the Lord's work."

Major Garside stood by his bit of window looking out toward the Gileadean quarters waiting for McCoy to reappear. McCoy had been there for quite a while. He felt a mounting annoyance. Abel kept puttering, waiting for him to come to his dinner which had already been postponed the hours since noon.

"Yo' just got to get your nourishment, Mist' Major, Sir," said Abel at last. "Yo' can't keep on goin' the way you have been. This venison, it ain't very fat nohow, and I'm just afraid, Mist' Major, that it'll get all dried out and tough. And I did so have my heart set on you havin' a good dinner."

"All right, Abel, I'll eat it now."

McCoy had come from the Gileadean hut, and Garside remained yet a while wishing to see his face—whether it had an expression of hope, discouragement, new resolve. It merely looked thin and tired. He walked straight past and disappeared inside Kavanaugh's. The Major then sat down and unfolded a napkin.

"I do hope that ain't dried-out tough," said Abel.

He ate, and Abel served him. Everyone else in the

camp fell-to and ate like hounds, but not the Major. It was a pleasure for Abel to watch the Major eat. *Dine.* It was impossible to serve a man who was not willing to dine. Abel always managed to have some tidbit that made dinner an occasion. In this instance it was a tart which he had made of meal, sugar, nutmeg, and deer shortening. It was the deer shortening which made all the difference.

"Ah, a cinnamon tart!" said Garside.

"Nutmeg, sir."

"Abel, you devil! How do you hide these things away?"

"It could do with just a sprightly bit more of sugar. Just a sparkle of loaf sugar grated on top."

"It's very good, Abel."

Abel had served the tart early in hopes the Major would leave some of the venison.

"Mist' Major, sir. There goes that McCoy again. It looks like he's startin' out on another hunt."

Garside, using a napkin on fragments of tart, went to the window and saw that McCoy had his rifle and blanket-roll, but no snowshoes. That meant he was not going back toward the mountains where the snow was deep and soft. He was obviously heading down one of the coulees where Bethel and the Zellner woman had gone in the foolish attempt to snare grouse for the blood-cure.

"My fur-lined coat, fresh sox, rifle!" he said to Abel who was whining about so much of dinner being left and at the same time looking at the left-over venison with greedy eyes. "Snap to it!"

Garside left, walking. He turned north from the gate, traveling in a direction almost opposite that taken by McCoy. He inspected the woodlot and kept going until the coulee hid him; then only did he change his course and turn south in a wide circle that would either intercept McCoy or cut his trail. He inspected his rifle, and kept an oil plug in the muzzle. He saw that the cartridges were lubricated, but very lightly. In cold weather it was best to use only the merest skiff of oil from the brain of venison, or the marrow.

I am taking a chance of Bethel hearing the shot, thought Garside. But one made a mistake in trying to be too absolutely safe. He had learned that in the war. When a thing had to be done it was best to go ahead and do it. Old Hulbush was not going to recover. With him dead, Bethel would look again at McCoy. And that son-of-a-bitching Klinkke to encourage her . . . He had ever-recognized the danger in Klinkke, in whose veins flowed something like a tannery solution of vitriolic acid. And then everything would go smash—all he had sacrificed and worked for, dumped out his capital and his sweat. Yes, and even his self-respect—bowing and fawning at the very behinds of those stupid Gileadeans.

He traveled north. A wind met him. It made him turn his head and keep his mitten up. It cut like nails. The sun was sucked up in a grayness, and a ground blizzard began to blow. The blizzard cast snow around his legs with a hissing sound.

Bethel and the Zellner woman would start home with the blizzard, and it would be his luck for them to meet McCoy. Garside watched for them when he climbed with slow effort to the crest of a knoll. There was no one. No one anywhere. No movement, or sound, except the snow around his legs, and his own breathing.

He walked for half an hour. When the snow flew very thick he judged distance by counting his steps to a hundred, a thousand. He descended a series of little flats and came to a broad coulee. It was so wide that its opposite cutbank-side was a vague line through the storm. Brush marked the stream bed, and where side gullies entered there were groves of small trees.

The snow was deep at the foot of the cutbank. He waded to his waist, crossed to the middle of the coulee, and kept to slightly higher ground edging some brush. It was easier to walk there; and the snow was soft and only about to his knees. He seldom left the fort, and he now realized the need for the snowshoes the men had been making of bent cottonwood and resin-boiled rawhide.

Someone was coming. He drew his rifle from its protective fur covering, made sure it was loaded, removed the plug of greased cloth from its muzzle.

The man was coming through the brush. Yes, he knew McCoy well enough—the way he carried his rifle, the way he strode along. An arrogant man, one not to take even the hint of a torn-apart face, member of the Eastern barnyard aristocracy: the landed gentry, the people who had treated Garside like dirt underfoot in his youth, in the years when he was an orphan bound-boy, an apprentice. It is too bad, thought Garside, that I cannot meet him with the gun muzzle, a final understanding, moment of triumph. But it added to the chance, however slightly. It was a mark of character to ignore such petty considerations.

He waited until the range was right. Particularly shooting against the wind, the bullet had a tendency to wander. He waited until his quarry was about eighty yards off, coming straight toward him, head down. Then he brought the sights on and squeezed the trigger.

The rifle recoiled with a good feeling against his shoulder. Everything seemed to work more slowly because of the storm. The man was hit but he was a moment in going down, as if his heavy clothes and the snow held him. Then he did not fall really, but turned and settled in, and he lay with his back showing, a dark hump, and the storm between them like fog.

Garside took time to look up and down the coulee. He saw with satisfaction that the tracks he had made only a minute or two before were filling with snow. He made ready with a second cartridge in case McCoy was not quite dead. But in approaching he received a shock. A shawl had been around the man's shoulders and had come loose to lie across the snow. For an instant he thought he had killed a woman. But it was a man, bearded. He rolled him over realizing with a sudden annoyance and anger that it was not McCoy. It was a Gileadean—Nephi Zellner.

"Oh, you son-of-a-bitch," he whispered through his teeth. "You meddling son-of-a-bitch."

Zellner had removed his round hat, otherwise he'd have recognized him as a Gileadean. He had put it inside his coat, and now it was lying beside him, half filled with snow.

"Fool!" whispered Garside. "You went looking for your woman and were killed for it. You humbling fool."

When he returned through darkness to the fort he found the Gileadeans assembled and praying.

"Has Sister Hulbush returned?" he asked Klinkke.

"No, but Sister Zellner was found, praise be to God."

"Is there a search party out?"

"Only Brother Nephi. We pray for him, and for Sister Hulbush."

"When did Sister Zellner come in?" he asked, alarmed that she might have seen him, or heard the shot, and later . . .

177

"Her husband guided her to the squawman's shanties. Then he traveled back to her directions knowing where it was she should meet Sister Hulbush. He would have met her before dark surely. We pray that they survive this stormy night."

Garside did not dare send even his own men for fear his tracks might yet be seen in the snow and identified leading from Zellner's body. He found Sister Zellner and tried to learn where her rendezvous with Bethel was to take place, but all she could recall were some general directions related to Denker's where she had last seen her husband.

"He will find her, Sister," said Klinkke. "Have no fear of that. They will survive this night in the tempest and come in safe and secure on the morrow. Brother Garside, will you join us in prayer?"

But Garside was too embittered with God to entreat Him in prayer. He went into the night, thinking of the immensity of his sacrifice—guiding these who claimed to be His chosen people, tying up his capital, ripping a season of the most brutal effort from his life, even reading the Bible and attending prayer—and in payment for all this, the ugly trick that the fates had played on him!

CHAPTER 6

MCCOY WAS FAMILIAR WITH THE COULEES LEADING northward from the fort. When he heard that Bethel and the Zellner woman had gone out for grouse, he knew their most likely goal. It was a place where two coulees met, making a mile or more of flat ground with bullberries, chokecherries, and rose thorn, and where

178

grouse wintered by the hundreds. The women were not there, but he found a man's tracks and followed them.

It was growing dark when he almost fell over Zellner's body. He found him shot with his body still warm, and he saw the dim impression of Garside's tracks.

It did not occur to him whose tracks they were, or that the bullet which killed Zellner had been meant for him. For some reason he thought the tracks belonged to Denker, but why Denker would want to kill this man he couldn't guess. Then it occurred to him that the same man who murdered Zellner might be waiting for him, so he retreated into the brush, crossed the snow-filled slot of the creek, and walked back down the other side toward the grouse country. When it was too dark to see a tree in front of him he stopped in some shelter against a clay bank, made himself as comfortable as he could with branches around his shoulders and dead leaves around his patched boots, and waited out the night.

In the morning, during a brief lull in the storm, he saw a figure slow-moving in some misty bushes to the northwest. He fired his gun and the movement stopped. He called and received no answer and the storm closed in again. He ran, and slowed, and tried to keep steadily to a course. He wished for a compass. He had nothing but the wind to guide him. An hour later he found some tracks, depressions filling with snow. He got down, brushing and blowing the loose flakes away. They were boot tracks, and quite small. He was certain they were Bethel's.

The tracks led him gently curving southwestward away from the coulees, and away from the fort also, across the snow on a course that could lead only to the wilderness of the Big Horns. He followed for hours, but intermittently because for whole quarter-mile stretches they would be blanked out by snow. He crossed a barren valley and the ice of a river. He walked across barren high ground for hours. Then it was early twilight, he roused from a half-dream, and the tracks were fresh, less than an hour old, and they led down into a rocky little canyon where some pine trees grew. He started to call out, heard the crash of movement through naked brush, and saw her.

He descended, calling her name. She came slowly, pushing the wire-hard twigs aside. She wore a wool robe which covered her head and was fastened under her chin, and her face looking out seemed perfectly calm, only curious. She tripped over a buried branch and fell, and her strength seemed to run out. But her voice was calm.

"Did you come from the fort?" she asked.

"Yes. Are you all right?" He was afraid her feet might be frozen. If they were he had to get her boots off in a hurry and rub some circulation into them.

"How far is it?"

"I don't know." He pressed her feet. "Can you feel that? Does that hurt?"

"Yes. No, it doesn't hurt. I thought I heard them chopping wood at the fort."

"It's too far. We've gone all day to the west. I think we've crossed over the divide to the Yellowstone."

"But that can't be. I followed the coulee."

"This country is so low it fools you. We might be as much as twenty miles from the fort. When the storm lifts we can see the mountains and get a landmark."

"Where's Erna?"

"Mrs. Zellner?"

"Yes. She was to meet me. I walked and walked."

"They'll have a search party out. I'm sure she's all right."

He didn't want to frighten her by telling about Zellner.

"What will we do?" she asked.

"Just stay alive, until the storm's over."

Darkness was settling. He looked about for a cave in the sides, an out-thrust strata, a bank where the snow had not come—but all was billowing in deep white. Fallen trees lay everywhere covered by snow. He managed to trample a smooth place among dead trees against a bank and construct a lean-to with pine branches for roof and floor.

When he finished it was dark. He knew Bethel was beside him only by the sounds she made.

"I can't build a fire," he said. "This deadwood is all frozen with the snow in it. Tomorrow, maybe, I'll find some juniper. It burns like turpentine. Here, I have some food."

He had some frozen venison left, and a few flat slabs of Mrs. Kavanaugh's pounded-root hardtack. The venison, although raw, was the more edible. Frozen, it broke across the grain of the muscles and it thawed in chewing, leaving a sweetish taste.

"That's all for now," he said.

"I'm hungry. Please, I'm starving. I have to have more." She frantically felt and tore at the small parfleche, at his clothing, and even looked in the lean-to to find where he might have hidden it. "Please, I'm starving."

He held her by the arms until she stopped and was able to control herself.

"I'm sorry," she said. "I don't know what came over me."

181

"Eat too much of this stuff and it's worse than none at all. After a while we'll have a bit more."

"Yes. I'm sorry."

"It happens to everybody."

"Not to you."

"Maybe I've eaten already."

Alone on the trail a man had to ration himself or die. It was just himself against himself. In a group it was one man against another to see who would get the most. Good men would turn to sneak thieves and killers when the food madness was on them. And you never knew which man it would be. For instance, between Denker and Aldo Rimmel, you'd naturally think it would be Denker who'd turn wolf, grab, fight, devour, or turn cannibal. But it might not be. It could as easily be big, decent Rimmel. So the sudden loss of control by the girl surprised him, but it shouldn't have.

"I'm really not so hungry now," she said.

The lean-to formed a back and head shelter, but when a person tried to lie on the blanket the cold came up from the earth. They had to sit and seek warmth from the close, snow-packed roof, and from each other's bodies. Sleep was a succession of nightmare-dozings. McCoy stood up whenever he felt his feet going dead, and he got the girl up with him. When she would not rise willingly, he shook her and made her get to her feet, and he kept her walking back and forth in the packed snow in front of the lean-to. Later, toward morning, he slept more deeply and was aroused by a noise in the bushes.

He went out with his rifle. Wolf tracks were around. He had hoped for a shot at a deer. Disappointed, he came back and managed to find pitchbark and build a fire.

He melted snow and thawed willow bark until it could be peeled and, afterward, boiled to make a bitter tea. They boiled some of the venison, and ate it with the root-cakes. A pale sunlight lay across an unfamiliar land. Some blue peaks rose to the south. Their lower slopes were in timber. A river, or what seemed to be river, cut a deep gash terminating the bench and the mountain highland to the west. He was completely lost. He had no idea what river it was, or the tributary to what river. It descended into what had the look of a game country.

"This isn't the way," said Bethel.

"No, but it will take us to higher country. Maybe we can see the fort."

Does she expect me to deliver her back to Garside? he wondered. Anyway, the barrens they had covered was a frigid route of death. To the west lay a new country, abundant, so he hoped, and with the camps of Yellowstone and Bozeman City beyond.

They left the gulch and the wind got a sweep at them. A peculiar coarse and tassled grass protruded from the snow. The bench, when they reached it, proved actually a series of undulations leading down to several gulches. He chose what seemed to be the largest gulch and descended. There was abundant grass and a deer trail. Conifers grew on the hillsides and aspen lower down. The deer trail went on and on. Animals had been over it since morning. He saw glossy droppings, uncoated by frost.

In the late afternoon they reached a small stream hidden under two feet of snow. When they stood very quiet the deep running of water could be heard. There was an icy hole in the snow from which a sulphur-smelling vapor rose. The vapor turned dense white before disappearing in the winter air. Hot springs dotted miles of the valley, and the cold seemed to diminish as if through the subcutaneous heating of the land. In a mile there was a cluster of springs, the melted slits of hot, running water, and several steaming ponds. Bubbles the size of one's fist rose through the ponds and burst to smell like decayed potatoes. Some huts had been built nearby—igloo and pyramid shapes covered with bark, slabs of which remained in place—apparently the steam houses of Indians.

Using a flat scoop of the frozen bark, McCoy unearthed more poles and bark from the snow. He found it possible to fit the bark like large shingles and smear it with mud from the pond which set hard in the cold. By evening he had a solid shelter and Bethel scraped the last remnant of snow from inside, and he built a fire.

After days of cold the heat seemed like a drug. They cooked and devoured the last bit of food. When it was gone, they looked at each other by the smoky firelight.

She is beautiful, thought, McCoy. She is young, and strong, and beautiful. He had been fed, and strength ran warm through his body. His wants were only half cared for. He wanted her. He was drawn to her compellingly. He caught her with groping hands and she fought away from him.

"Bethel!" For a while all he could think of was her name. He put his arms around her knees and pressed his head against them. She had backed to the limits of the hut. "Bethel!" and he tried to pull her beside him.

"No!"

Suddenly angered by rejection, he cried, "What is it? Is it Garside? Is that the reason? Are you saving yourself to be next woman in bed for Garside?"

She didn't answer, but he demanded an answer. He

184

would have used violence to get an answer.

"Is it? Is he the one you're saving yourself for?"

"It's as it has to be!" she cried out.

"Why? Why *has* to be?"

"You wouldn't understand. What is God or faith to you? What is my family to you? You don't understand. You don't want to understand."

He stared at her dumbly, like an animal wanting her.

"We have to go back!" she said.

"To *him*!"

She did not answer.

"To him. To Garside. Say it. I have to take you back to Garside!"

"I will go alone."

"Say you love him and I'll take you back."

She would not.

"You don't care for him."

"What has that to do with it?"

"What has a woman's love for a man to do with marriage? Even the Gileadeans . . ." He checked himself.

"Even!" she said.

"I'm sorry."

"We marry, and love comes."

"Garside?"

"Yes, maybe! I hope so. Yes! Yes, it is best. Our people need him. He will be the new prophet, the one seen in vision. The one we have prayed for."

"Garside a prophet!" and he had to laugh.

"How would you know? You don't *believe*."

"Does he believe?"

"He says he believes. Isn't a man's simple statement enough?"

"I think a fellow like Garside should have to prove it."

"I am going back. If you won't go back with me I'll find my way alone."

"All right, I'll go back. But right now we're out of food. There's game. And trout in the creek, maybe, if we can chop through the ice. We have fire and shelter. In a few days we can go north. To the Yellowstone. These creeks have to lead somewhere. Then we can get a rescue party together. Food for all of them, your people and mine."

"I must go back," she said. "Before Papa dies."

"Bethel, I saw him. He can't live more than a few days."

"He will live. I have to go back. It will be warmer tomorrow. I will pray to God that food be sent us. I will pray."

"And what of me?"

She stared at him.

"What of me? Don't you know that I love you? Didn't I let you know that long enough ago? And you love me. I'm the man you *want*. I'm the man you want to go with, stay with, live with. You want to be the mother of my children. Good God, you don't want to have that monster's spawn growing inside you."

"Keep quiet!" she cried.

"Tell me it isn't true, then I'll be quiet."

"Leave me alone." She sat down in the spruce boughs and turned away from him. "Leave me alone, leave me alone."

She refused the blanket and slept half-sitting in the spruce boughs. He studied her face in the dying firelight. Asleep she looked younger, almost like a little girl. He felt a great, warm sympathy for her. He resolved not to take her back. He would use any ruse or

186

delay to keep her from returning. The wind had begun to blow, thumping a loose end of bark and making a bass aeolian sound through the poles projecting from the smokehole. He felt alarm that it might be a chinook wind—warm, from the southwest, a break in winter. But the wind came through the smokehole carrying a fine powder of snow, and the hut was cold on the north side. The wind continued rising and falling with a moan, pushing smoke into the hut and sucking it out again, and the fire alternately sank and burned cracking yellow.

He woke up, the fire low, the girl on her side moaning from the cold. He covered her and went outside for fuel. It was dark without a star. He tore down one of the old sweat houses but he had no axe to break the poles. He had to drag them inside and lay them across the fire so they would burn through. Afterward he fed them inward and they shortened steadily as the night wore on.

He fell asleep sitting by the fire. He was chilled through when he awoke, and Bethel was up, on one knee, looking at him.

"You are like ice," she said, touching him.

"I'm all right."

"You gave me the blanket after all. You sleep now and I'll watch the fire."

He lay where she had been and the turf and spruce boughs held the heat of her body. The spruce smelled of her. He shivered violently, and his teeth chattered. It seemed to frighten her and she lay over him, helping him with her warmth. Her body was rigid but she allowed him to put his arms around her and hold her close.

"Bethel!" he said, trying to take her, but her reaction was violent. For a second she was like a mountain cat fighting against him, and she burst free and rose as far

187

as her knees. The boughs tangled her, and her head touched the poles of the slanting roof. He said "Bethel!" again, desperately, and held her with his arms around her waist, his face pressed hard against her abdomen. And she stopped there, not giving herself, but not fighting him away further. Her hands took him by the beard, her fingers in his hair. She did not hate him but she did not bend further.

"Bethel, why are we here? Hasn't God thrown us together? Isn't it through His will?" He thought, this is what Garside would say. But the thing was he meant it. Yes, it was true. "What could it have been, but God's will that stopped your wedding, took you away, put us together. I didn't know the way here. I never saw the country before. But something guided me. Us."

"No. It can't be. It can never be."

"Why?"

"Because I was born *me*. I have my faith. My people."

"You can keep your faith, Bethel. I'm not a farmer, I'll never be a farmer, but I won't bar you from your people. These things will work out."

"No."

"In the name of God, the God who cast us together I take you as my wife, Bethel. I, Morgan McCoy, take you, Bethel Hulbush as my wife. Say the same. Say it. Say 'I, Bethel Hulbush, take you, Morgan McCoy, as my husband.' In any religion, it will be a valid marriage. Even the Jesuits. And your faith, too. It must be. It would have to be."

But she would not say it. She shook her head and sobbed with the intensity of not saying it, and she got up, and left him, and built up the fire.

He was left with a residue of frustration, hunger, cold.

He thought he might be getting a fever. He slept, and she sat by him. When he woke up she was asleep and had given him half the blanket. The fire was coals under a feather of ash. Light came through the smokehole and between the slabs of bark. The hut shook under repeated impacts of the wind. He went outside for wood. There was no traveling anywhere in such a wind. The land was a white wilderness.

They ate the final bits of meat, and drank sweetish bark-tea. After laying up heaps of firewood, McCoy took his rifle and went out into the storm. He crossed the creek and looked for places where deer might seek cover in groves of aspens, at the cirque ends of little draws. He walked all day and came back tired and cold. From somewhere Bethel had dug some roots which, pounded and boiled, made a starchy, soda-flavored gruel. He slept, and, awaking in the dark, with the whimper sounds of wolves about, set out to kill one. He fired and hunted for the warm carcass. There was no sign of it, no blood, only tracks vanishing in the snow. He walked, and daylight came. He was in a part of the valley he had not seen before. Grass grew with unusual abundance and there was good shelter. The snow had been packed in places by bedded animals. He caught the smell of them. He came to a steep little bank and almost fell in descending it. Grass grew to his armpits. Suddenly there were rising, brownish shapes all around. Elk were bedded down, ten, a dozen, or fifty of them. He turned, aimed point-blank, and fired. A big animal was down. Its front legs seemed to have buckled and he could see eyes and antlers and rear quarters above the snow. Then it came directly toward him. He tried to lever a second cartridge but cold locked the gun. He tried to retreat but the deep grass and snow held him.

Then the great form crashed over him and he was driven down, down, and he felt the rough grass in his face and the coldness of snow.

He did not completely lose consciousness. He held the picture of the whitish belly-hair over him. He even remembered the oily hair smell. And afterward he heard the hoofs, or felt them through the ground. Frozen ground will carry vibration like the head of a drum. He was perfectly all right, but he felt different. It came to him that he was unable to move. There was no terror in this because he felt that he could move if he willed it. He felt that he could get up whenever he liked, only he was too tired.

A peculiar singing sound came and went. It seemed to pass repeatedly along his body. He amused himself by listening to it. Later he seemed to rock gently. Then he slept.

It might have been days or hours later that he woke up and wondered if his legs were frozen. It was then he tried to move and could not. He had the feeling of being suspended away from all solidity. If he could only find something firm for his elbows, hip, shoulder—even the back of his head—to give the initial push, then he could roll over and stand and walk. But the snowy grass seemed to hold him like a spiderweb.

"Bethel!" he called. The snow and grass closed his voice. It was without echoes. He had the feeling that it could not be heard a dozen feet away. "Bethel, Bethel!" he kept shouting at his own terror.

After a while he became tired, the singing sound commenced again and he sank back into a cold, suspended lethargy. Pain came to him. He ached in every fiber, but if he lay without thinking, without so much as breathing, it almost went away. I am freezing to death, he thought. I have always heard that a person feels warm when he is freezing, but that is untrue. I am freezing and these are the last thoughts I will ever have. It was remarkably easy to die. It was the slip-of-nothing.

Then he heard his name being called. He lay quietly listening to his name. He was loath to answer. It was like being awakened from his bed when he was a boy back in Ohio. His mother would call Morgan! and he would try not to hear her. He would roll over and clutch at the last delicious fragment of sleep.

The voice was nearer. "Morgan!" He could feel the impact of movement. "Morgan?" said her voice going away.

"Here!" He said it.

He could feel and hear her, one and the same; she bumped against him wading the deep snow. He could smell her—an odor of woodsmoke and the perfume of her body. She was trying to lift him. He sat up on hips that were like a frozen hinge.

"Morgan!" she kept saying, driving at his consciousness. She slapped his face. He could feel it along his spine, but his flesh was numb. After a while she got down and began rubbing his arms and legs. She took off his boots. The toes and heels of his sox had long since disappeared and he had been wrapping his feet in the rags cut in strips, and padding them with dry grass. She took his feet in her lap and warmed one with her abdomen while rubbing the other. After a while they started prickling, and the prickling mounted to a cold fire.

"Are they frozen?" she asked.

"I don't think so."

She pressed her hands hard against his feet and removed them to see whether the blood came back.

She put his boots back on. "You have to stand."

He stood with her help. He kept falling in the snow. He walked; afterward she pulled him on a rude travois. Then in the shanty, after chills and dreaming, he found her holding a hot drink to his lips. He fell asleep, suffered repeated chills and nightmares, and woke up with the shanty empty and the fire low. Later she was there and giving him a fat-beaded broth.

"Where did you get the meat?" he asked.

"It was the elk you shot."

She had found its frozen carcass, thawed it over a fire, quartered it, swung the haggled sections from the branches of trees, and dragged a neck and shoulder portion to the hut.

She rubbed his chest with some of the fat. A strip of lean was roasting on a stick propped over the fire. He seized the meat and ate it, suddenly ravenous, and wanted more. He would have fought for more, but the meat was gone, and he fell back exhausted. After a while he felt sick. The meat had become a lump in his stomach. He became cold, colder than he had ever been in his life. The fire's warmth seemed to pour through the smokehole. All it did was pull in the cold air. He started to shiver. He dreamed and sat up in bed. He saw a wolf standing just inside the door. It was a great gray-black animal with bristly hair. I am imagining it, he thought. I have a fever. But the wolf stood there, and he could see its yellowish fangs and the slather of foam at the corner of its mouth. Bethel had hold of him, but he twisted with a madman's strength and lunged for his rifle which was leaning on a heap of firewood across the hut. She hurled the rifle out of his reach and he dived again for it.

Finally he burned his leg in the fire and the pain made

him realize he was dreaming.

"I'm sorry!" he said to her, getting some control.

"You have a fever."

"Yes, of course."

The wolf kept reappearing, but with the sane half of his mind he ignored it, saying it was a dream. He sat down on the floor, too weak to get back to the bed. Sweat poured from him, and afterward he got cold and had the shakes. With Bethel's help he returned to the bed.

"Do you feel better?" she asked.

"I'm cold, cold." He wanted to say something else, but all he seemed able to do was shiver and say the word, "Cold . . ."

She did not dare move him to the warm side of the fire because the smoke gathered in a blue, choking haze. When she added more fuel the smoke thickened. She packed boughs against the wall and lay down beside him to warm him with her own body. She lay half-supporting his weight, and she could feel the beating of his heart. After a while he stopped trembling, his teeth no longer chattered, and he slept.

She awoke from his movements. The fire had gone down but the bed was not cold. They were secure against cold as long as they did not disturb the nearness of their bodies. She thought, I have to get up, I must build the fire. But she did not move. She lacked the will and the strength to move. He was saying "Bethel, Bethel," in her ear, and seeking. She made no resistance as he removed her heavy Gileadean skirts. He lay on her and she bore him. I must tell him I am his wife, she thought. I must say the words, "I, Bethel Hulbush. . ." But she forgot all about the words. She forgot everything but the fullness of having him, and afterward she shielded him from the ground. They lay together in the closest embrace, the winter locked out, all desolation and doubt closed away forever.

CHAPTER 7

THE STORM CONTINUED WITH BRIEF LAPSES FOR TWO days. Then it cleared, and became very cold. All but the very apexes above the springs froze. Vapor rose through chimneys of ice, and the ice built up until each spring looked like a miniature volcano.

Testing the creek ice for airholes, McCoy located places where warm currents flowed, leaving it only a few inches thick. He used a sharp fragment of quartzite to chop through and get water for drinking. Later he fished for trout which were a welcome change to the all-elk diet.

Sometimes he would glimpse himself in the water, a bearded stranger. Bethel fashioned a comb of horn, and he barbered himself using a knife honed to razor-keenness.

With food in plenty, the living became routine. It left many hours to spend. They devised games. He carved rude counters and learned to play Gileadean checkers. Through many hours they lay together, and lost all embarrassment of their naked bodies. Often whole long segments of afternoon would be spent locked in their mated embrace, dozing, waking only at intervals, and sleeping without parting after moments of fulfillment.

Days passed one into another, with no calendar except the changes of the moon. The evening light began to linger.

One morning McCoy walked to the creek and looked at a sky which had turned a dread, liverish-gray. A wind moved unsettled through the high spruce trees. It was a switching wind, first northwest, then northeast, and snow was carried over the ridge on a misty ground blizzard. The wind gathered strength; it turned and blew from the southwest; it felt frigid, but everywhere the snow was changing in luster. The snow clotted underfoot and dripped through the roof of the shanty. Ridge crests appeared. All the great country seemed to be awaking and rising through the snow. An Indian trail emerged and could be seen distantly skirting the valley, looping down and down toward the land of the Yellowstone. Streams ran under the deep snows of the gulches. They spread water over the bottoms and the still-solid creek ice so anyone who attempted to cross from one side to the other would find himself thigh-deep in slush, but with hard footing beneath. It was a chinook wind, famed breaker of the northern winters—so called because it swept in from the land of the Chinook Indians.

Only the lees of gulches and the timberland held heavy snow when the chinook blew itself out. It was still February, by McCoy's calculations, but the back of winter had been broken. There continued to be a hard freeze every night, but under the sun of afternoon the paths and the roof would steam.

They made preparations to leave. McCoy repaired his boots with the back hide of elk, cured with natural acid from the sulphur springs, and hung in the smokehole. A supply of jerky was made by slow drying on poles over the fire.

Setting out one morning before dawn, they traveled steadily and came down onto the wide Yellowstone valley at sundown—a distance of about thirty-five miles. They met two white men, bearded and with hair to their shoulders—prospectors who had wintered with the Crows. One of them gallantly let Bethel ride his horse, the men alternating with the second mount, and they reached Yellowstone City after nightfall next day.

The town was a clutch of shacks and frame-front buildings standing on a bench of gravelly earth above the river. It was the place at which both the Bozeman and Bridger routes joined, and where men from the gold camps came to build mackinaw boats in which to float through all the wild Sioux country to Missouri.

McCoy entered the town with some trepidation after his brush with vigilantes the autumn before, but his beard and scar-changed face were sort of a disguise.

However, he was instantly recognized by the storekeeper.

"You should have hung around," he said, showing no animosity. "Well, maybe you shouldn't have, but you should have come back. Those fellows calling themselves vigilantes got cleaned out by the U.S. Marshals."

"What do you mean 'cleaned out'?"

"When I say cleaned out I mean mostly dead. The Wickhorst boys were—one shot and one hung. A fellow named Joe Banks got hung right out of town here. He was wanted for horse stealing at Orofino. I think they hung Tronson and McKibbon, too, but it was never admitted. You know how marshals are. They hold political jobs and if you hang a man and forget it he's just as dead, and it doesn't make the hard feelings."

Through most of winter Yellowstone City had been isolated as completely as Fort Hunter. Fully a tenth of its population had died, most of them the victims of a lung fever, and they lay in boxes in a coulee back of town waiting for the ground to thaw. Prices were very high. Flour was up to $90 a hundred, with lard, sugar, molasses, and dried fruits somewhat more. Buffalo meat, however, was twenty cents, and good jerky, grease-packed in parfleche containers, twenty-five. Whisky at $1.50 a quart was the cheapest thing in camp—Yellowstone's eight saloons having all laid in large stocks of both keg and bottled goods—but only the storekeeper had thought of food.

There was a U.S. Commissioner, who also presided over a justice court, and performed marriages. McCoy knew that Bethel considered herself his wife, and her Gileadean belief accorded no validity to a civil marriage, but he preferred giving their union a legality before returning to Fort Hunter. Therefore, the marriage was performed. Yellowstone City staged a dance, and afterward, in the hotel room of the bridal couple, beat tin pans in the traditional charivari.

Next day McCoy went around town, securing goods and horses on credit for their return to Fort Hunter. When he returned to Bethel she surprised him by a sudden pleading not to return, but to go on— somewhere, anywhere—northwestward among the gold camps. The outburst was a surprise, but he realized what a day-by-day change had taken place in her.

"You're afraid of Garside," he said.

She looked at him without denying it.

"I'm afraid of him, too. But there's no use running. We'll go back to Hunter and face him. You're my wife now. There's nothing he can do about that."

"He can kill you."

"No, I don't believe he'll kill me."

He'd said he was afraid, but once the decision was

197

made he was afraid no longer.

They left on the fourth day, but McCoy was $700 in the storekeeper's debt and owed almost as much to the keeper of a corral. However they were decently mounted, and led two packhorses laden with flour, lard, dried apples, jerky, and smaller foods—including ten pounds of hard candy and several quarts of Kentucky whisky.

They followed the army road which was a pair of ruts filled with crunch-ice. It could be seen afar like a strip of frothy glass through the remnant snow and brown of the country.

There had been no reports of Indian trouble. The Crows were generally friendly, and the treaty had at least temporarily quieted the Cheyennes. The Snakes and their more warlike cousins, the Bannocks, were said to be wintering far south toward the Popo Agie. A single rider appeared along some coulee rims. He appeared and disappeared throughout the afternoon. Fearing he was a scout for some Crow village, they unsaddled and cooked at a fire-gutted Army way-station; and when night settled, before the moon rose, quietly left and made a cold-camp some five miles further along. But the prairie night, marvelous for listening, carried no sound except the coyotes and wolves, and no movement anywhere.

Next day the rider appeared again, and McCoy, with his hand lifted in a sign of peace, left Bethel with the packhorses and rode toward him. To his surprise the man waited. It proved to be Ignatius Denker.

Ignatius seemed to have recovered from his abdominal wound. He returned McCoy's sign, but did not offer to shake hands. He considered himself Indian rather than white. His eyes showed no flicker of friendship, either. Only a dark interest.

"How are things at the fort?" asked McCoy.

He dipped his head indicating they were the same. He then spoke in monosyllables supplemented by sign language: There was a shortage of food . . . A total of six had died.

"Who?"

He named two of the Gileadeans—a man and a woman—Mrs. Bowers, young Jim McFadden, old Baldwin, and Babcock, who had been employed by Garside.

"How about Hulbush?"

He shrugged.

"You mean he's still alive?"

He nodded.

"Good Lord!"

He did not want him dead, not really, only it would have been so much easier for Bethel. That is, as long as he was bound to die in a few weeks anyhow.

"I suppose we were given up for dead?"

"Who is with you?"

He had not recognized her because of the bright plaid riding cloak which the boys in Yellowstone City had given her as a wedding present.

"Bethel Hul . . ." He said. "My wife. I married the Hulbush girl in Yellowstone City." For the first time there was a glint in the half-breed's eyes. But he made no comment, and the three rode on to the fort together.

Major Garside was napping in his quarters when an unusual excitement in the yard caused him to rise and look from the window. Someone had arrived with packhorses, and the Methodist end of the fort had gathered in a noisy, cheering audience when the sacks were dragged down. Then he saw Abel Tunis and called him in.

"What is it?"

"It's that renegade, McCoy. He come back again, Mist' Major. He must have been to a town someplace. He come in with all kinds of supplies."

Garside knew by his orderly's manner that this was not the whole of it. He waited while Tunis found the right words.

"He come in with Miss Hulbush, Mist' Major. She alive! Yes, sir, she alive and looking well-enough. Appears she didn't get froze after all. But she didn't stay with Mist' McCoy one minute after she hove through the gate. No, sir, she ran off straight to her father's."

Garside heard him with no change of expression. He knew that Tunis was watching for some sign, but he would not wince and give him his satisfaction.

"I'll shave now," he said.

"Yes, sir!"

He did not care to show himself before thinking exactly what he was going to do. At the outset he had seen it as more than a coincidence that McCoy and Bethel had disappeared on the same night. He could imagine Bethel becoming lost in the storm, but not McCoy—McCoy who had shown the day-after-day ability to live like a wolf, hunt for entire weeks at a time, get first bite at the liver and marrowbone rather than endure the root-cellar type of survival offered by the fort. They had obviously been together, sharing each other's robes. But even as he imagined Bethel on her back receiving him, he gave Tunis and his lathering brush only the reposed mask of his face.

"It's candy!" Children were yelling outside. He could

hear the voices of Gileadeans as well as the rest, all cheering the arrival of food. And Kavanaugh: "By Gawd, it's real, gen-u-wine Kentucky whisky!"

Shaved and combed, wearing a fresh shirt for which some of the camp's precious store of flour had been used as starch, he walked to the Gileadean house. He rapped sharply and waited with a military stiffness, and only a hint of impatience, to be let in. People were whispering, there was silence, Brother Samuel was alone in the passage, but others were peeping and waiting.

"Is Bethel here?"

"She is with her father," said Samuel.

He walked to the Hulbush quarters. She was not in the room. Hulbush, propped in bed, waited for him. He was a creature of parchment-over-bones, and his hands looked like the feet of a chicken, but a glow had appeared on his face.

"Ah, Brother Garside! You have heard?"

"Your daughter returned."

"Yes. Saved. An act of God. I have prayed for it. Again and again, waking in the dark . . ."

Garside listened for only a part of this and asked, "Where is she?" When the old man waved uncertainly he said, "This fellow McCoy, what about him?"

"Ah, my son, this is what saddens me. She is his wife."

"What do you mean *his wife*? You mean he got her in the robes when she couldn't help herself . . ."

"No, no! She took him as her husband. They joined hands and professed the marriage words in the hearing and in the sight of Almighty God."

"You mean, in your faith, that sort of a thing is a marriage?"

"It is not our usual marriage, as you know. But it is a marriage in the eyes of the Lord."

Hulbush reached to impart a grasp of comfort with one of his rooster hands, all yellowish skin and great nails, but Garside moved back from him.

"Ah, I feel for you in your disappointment," said Hulbush. "And it is my sadness, also. You know how I sought that you two would be wed. But the will of God was otherwise. Let us not stand against the will of God, Brother. Please rejoice that we have her back alive and well."

"Where is she?"

"I will call."

"Never mind." He did not want the old fool with his parrot voice and holy-Jehovah rantings to intrude. He wanted to see her alone.

He went from the door and stood in the runway that the weather had warmed, now empty of mules and chickens. Several women watched him. Then Bethel walked toward him alone.

She walked directly on with her head up, and did not avoid his gaze. She did not fear him. Her mettle appealed to him. He knew then that, God's marriage or not, he was going to make her his wife. If she truly regarded this adventure in the robes as a marriage, then he would have her as a widow.

"Did he tell you?" she asked.

"He told me. I understand how it was. But you promised to be my wife, Bethel!"

"But now it cannot be."

"It can! You're not legally his wife."

"I *am* legally his wife."

He stared at her.

"We were married by magistrate in Yellowstone City."

202

It was a blow to him. "You're a religious girl! What do the words of a magistrate mean?"

"He is my husband. He was my husband already. It has happened. It wasn't the way I planned, but the way it had to be. I'm glad it was. I'm his wife. I'll always be his wife."

"Bethel." It was a masterpiece of control. He effected a warmth in his voice. He sounded emotion-filled, stricken not by anger but by sadness. "Bethel, you must forgive me, knowing how I care for you. I wanted you for my wife. Now you are lost to me always. You must understand my feeling. Tell me that you understand."

"I understand," she whispered. "I'm so sorry . . . the way it happened. But it had to be."

"Of course. It had to be."

He took her hand and pressed it once. Only once, but firmly, before turning away.

Garside had not taken charge of the supplies as he should have, nor dictated their distribution. He cursed his men—Dennis, Elwell, Cox—why had they not stopped the unpacking? But the excitement had been too great, and McCoy had lost no time in distributing his largess to friend and Gileadean alike. He saw it as a crevice in his authority that this fellow, now that he had the woman, might seek to widen his influence.

He stood in his house until it was dark—and stood without a candle for a while yet. He could hear the voices from Kavanaugh's, which was a sort of communal shelter, whooping loud from whisky. Their cries reminded him of the yapping of dogs. The Gileadeans talked about Almighty God and the soul, a piece of Him in everyone. How could one see a spark of God in scum such as these? Were they his equal?

Garside would as willingly concede equality to hogs.

He was very bitter, but there was a fine clarity to his thinking. It was no problem having McCoy killed, but Bethel must have no suspicion. He would have to kill McCoy and discredit him at the same time. The drunken celebration was most opportune. If it could be made to seem that McCoy had been killed in a filthy ruckus, the whisky for which he had himself furnished, all could be accomplished at one sweep.

He went outside. There were some stars, but no moon. He could not see Abel, but several of his employees were hanging around the front of the fort and he called Dennis over.

"Oh, hello, boss," said Dennis.

Dennis had once presumed to call him "Henry" and the next instant found himself on his back with a bruised jaw, but "boss" was acceptable. He was still Garside's second-in-command, a loud swagger when the Major was not around, and grovelingly obsequious when he was.

"I have a bottle of brandy inside." Dennis thought he was being asked to drink with his master—the first time it had ever happened. However, Garside went on: "You're going to take it over to that wah-hoo they're staging in Kavanaugh's. Make out you stole it from me."

Dennis waited to learn what was up. "Yah?"

"I don't know whether McCoy is there or not. He'll be somewhere around. I'll have Abel come for him. After he's gone for about ten minutes, start a fight. It ought to be easy to do. Only I want it to be a big one. A real free-for-all."

"You want me to go in there and start a ruckus all alone?"

"You're a pretty big man, and a tough one." He laid a hand on Dennis' shoulder, and could feel him grow because of it. "Not that I want you to get hurt. I don't. I need you too bad. But nobody gets hurt when he just tries to protect himself after things get to rolling. Take Elwell with you, but tell him nothing. He's not a fellow we can trust."

Dennis waited to hear why the timing and the fight were necessary, but he never asked questions of Garside.

"You have it all clear?"

"Yes, I take the brandy, wait ten minutes, and start a fight. I start one hell of a fight."

"But after Abel comes for him."

"About ten minutes after."

"Right! Good fellow." He called, "Abel!" and not finding his orderly, got the brandy himself. It was his last bottle.

"They'll laugh their pants off when I tell 'em I stole it off from you," said Dennis.

"That's fine. Give them a good laugh."

"Were you calling me, Mist' Major?" asked Abel. "I did think I heard my name called."

"What were you doing?"

"Just standing around."

"In the dark?"

"I was sort of listening to that drinkin' affair."

"You wanted to be invited in."

Abel did not answer.

"Well, why shouldn't they invite you in? Don't they want to drink with a colored man? Isn't that a peculiar thing, Abel? They may be lousy and haven't had a bath since August but they don't drink with colored men."

"Might be it's that they know I'm your man, Major,

completely and absolutely."

"Do they hate me so much—refusing a snort to somebody because he's loyal to his commanding officer?"

"We just in different camps, me and them."

"You're a good man, Abel."

"Yes, sir, Mist' Major. I try and be."

"When this is all over, when we've sent this drunken scum over to their gold camps, and delivered these good, solid farming people to the valley, I'm going to see that you're rewarded for all this, Abel."

This was a new Garside, and Abel's eyes became speculative in the dark. However, when he spoke it was in his usual servant's voice. "Yes, sir. Thank you. I never had the least doubt of that, Mist' Major."

"You can name what you want when that time comes, Abel. And if it's within my power I'll get it for you."

"Thank you, sir."

"I'd have told you all this before, at the pass, along the trail, when it looked like revolt, except you might have construed it as bribery. But you gave me a full measure of loyalty without it. I'm not the man to forget that."

"No, sir. You ain't that type, sir. I found that out about you, sir."

"You've never married, Abel. I have been thinking that when we reach the end of our journey you might wish to change that. One of the Gileadean women? Zellner's widow, for instance. A good woman, handsome, and a comfort in your bed, Abel. You would not object to a white woman? All colors are the equal in the sight of God."

"I'm glad to hear you say that, Mist' Major."

"There's only one thing standing between us and such

an accomplishment. One man. A man who would like to lead these good religious people north to the gold camps. I'm referring to McCoy. That man will have to be put out of the way. Do you understand what I mean?"

"I think so."

"This is like the Army. You recall how we had to hang certain men in the Army? Deserters, traitors, spies—mercifully done away with?"

"Yes, sir."

"The individual must always be sacrificed for the good of the group. We all know how one bad potato can spread its black-rot through a whole barrel."

"Yes, sir."

"I have a mission for you tonight, Abel. I want you to find McCoy. He's at Kavanaugh's, I believe. Tell him Ignatius Denker wishes to speak to him on a very private matter. Tell him Ignatius is waiting for him in the cache house. He will think it has something to do with his sister. Let him assume that if he asks."

"Is that all, sir? Just say that Ignatius . . ."

"No, follow him as discreetly as you can. I'll need some help—afterward."

"Yes, sir."

Garside did not wish to go heavily weighted, so he left his Navy with its belt and holster, taking only his small double-gun. Chiefly he armed himself with a strap-iron bludgeon. It weighed a couple of pounds, was about eighteen inches long, and had one end broken off with a jagged edge. The strap iron was ideal because, after delivering the death blow, the edge could be used to place on McCoy the gouges and lacerations that men almost always receive in a brawl. If all went well when the fight started, his bludgeoned body would already have been moved to the dark close outside Kavanaugh's door. However, he did not make the mistake of planning too closely. The war had taught him better than that. One should keep his eye on the objective. The best plan was a general one with room to improvise and maneuver.

McCoy had been watching when Garside returned from his visit to the Hulbush house.

"He looks like a bull moose on the prod," said Doc beside him.

"An old rogue percheron."

"You haven't heard the last of it from that fellow."

"What can he do?"

"I can think of several things he can do. Number one, make your wife a widow."

"No, that's not his style. Those people wouldn't follow him afterward. And Garside never does anything just from plain healthy anger and revenge. I'm the sort of a guy who thinks things through, Doc, that's why I always beat you at checkers. I've been thinking Garside through. Now, what to him is winning? And what is losing? What's he after? Bethel for his wife? Or just control of these Gileadeans so he can set up a town and control a trade route? I think it's the latter. I think the man is crazy for position. That's why he goes on pretending to be a major after the war's over. Puts on that starched shirt every night. And he's after money, which means power. And position."

They watched Garside go inside his house. It was settling twilight, but no candle went on. Everyone everywhere was rejoicing, but the Major was by himself—by his window perhaps, watching, listening.

McCoy thought of going to see Bethel, but the other Gileadeans filled him with dread; then Doc wanted him

208

to go to Kavanaugh's, so he did.

The place was dense with heat, smoke, noise, and the smell of whisky. Aldo Rimmel saw him and dragged him over where a noisy argument was in progress. Was genuine Kentucky bourbon whisky made of corn, rye, or barley?

"It's made from corn."

They passed him a cupful. He stood with it, not wanting to carry a whisky breath in to see Elder Hulbush. Later when he turned to the door he was surprised to see Abel Tunis. Abel had come just inside, and was standing in the dimness watching him.

"Hello, Abel. Have you had a drink?"

"You didn't invite me."

"I didn't invite anybody. I just opened a bottle and they smelled it."

"Ha-ha! That certainly is a good joke, Mist' McCoy."

Obviously he was not looking for an invitation. His tenseness revealed itself in several ways; in his quick laugh, in his observant eyes.

"What is it, Abel?"

"Oh. Well, sir, Mist' McCoy, I got a message for you. I was supposed to bring you along, but very private-like."

"Over to headquarters? Is that where the deed is to be done?"

His joking remark seemed to touch Abel like a hot iron. "Oh, ha-ha! The *deed!* Well, I admit that Mist' Major he was a mite put out, but as for doing anything . . . there's not much he *can* do now you and Mis' Bethel is married. No, it ain't the Major wantin' to see you. He's in his quarters and I wouldn't think of disturbing him."

In the noise Abel found himself shouting, so he

209

backed from the door, privately gesturing McCoy to follow him.

"It's young Denker. You know, Ignatius?"

"What does he want?"

"That, Mist' McCoy, sir, I don't exactly know. I don't know, what to think about young Mist' Denker. He been acting so *strange*. You know how shy he's been about coming to the fort since . . . you know."

"Since the Major shot him."

"Major Garside he wouldn't think of harmin' him, not no more, and I told him that. But you just can't get him through the gate, hardly."

Ignatius had been hesitant about approaching the fort that evening, and finally came inside only far enough to unrope the packhorses.

"I do like the boy, and feel sorry for him. When he was layin' wounded down at his father's I sent him bowls of cold soup-jelly, hot poultices, all kinds of things. So he trusts me to come for you. But he wouldn't make a peep about what was upsetting him."

"Where is he?"

"Oh, he hid himself up in the cache house. He waitin' for you there."

Yes, thought McCoy, it's what Ignatius would do. He acted like a lone animal. Like a wolf, he preferred a den high in the coulee. As they walked toward the cache house he thought it was peculiarly like a den with its thick walls and little door. It was built of reclaimed sill logs—a small square hut with a pyramidal roof— standing on cottonwood piles to about the height of a man's head. The piles were covered with flattened tin cans to turn the claws of mice, packrats, skunks, even the bobcats and wolves that came in the night when the hunger was on. For months Garside had kept an armed

24-hour guard at the place, but now it was out of use, quiet, its door open, and there was a faint stink of rotten meat.

"I'll go talk to him and ask him to come over here if you'd like, Mist' McCoy. But I'm not at all sure it would do any good."

"No, he has some reason for hiding."

"Well, that's what *I* thought."

It did seem strange that he would send Abel. Unless, perhaps, because they were both dark-skinned. Negroes, he knew, were willingly taken in by many Indian villages which would exclude a white man.

It was dark and quiet. The whooping revelry at the big hut was rendered impersonal, and almost purified by distance. The Gileadeans were also having a time of it, and on the wind he caught an odor of baking pies. One of the Gileadeans walked past, quite close, carrying two buckets of water on a shoulder yoke. He waited until the man was at some distance before calling up to the little cache-house door.

"Ignatius! It's McCoy!"

Ignatius did not answer, but there was a responding movement. It was soundless, but there was a vibration of the house on its high, rather rickety piles. Like the tremble of a limb, which was the only hint of the lynx creeping along it.

"Ignatius? I'm alone. What did you want?"

The ladder did not reach the ground. It was held by pegs from above, and the first step was about eighteen inches high. Standing on the first step it was possible to raise one's head and shoulders inside the door. He wanted to show himself, but he did not want to stick his head up like a turkey at a shoot to be blown off at the shoulders in case it was Garside, or, more likely, one of his hired men.

He wished he had his gun. He had divested himself of its bulky weight at the house. He didn't have anything, not even a knife. He didn't need anything if it was Ignatius, of course, and if it wasn't he could drop to the ground, move under the house, and nobody could do a thing to him in the blackness.

He was not particularly suspicious. It would be Ignatius. Everything was in character with that strange youth, but as a precautionary feint, he took off his hat and coat, laid the coat across his bent forearm and placed his hat on top; then, climbing one-handed, he thrust the hat and false shoulders up into the opening. When nothing happened he felt like a fool, and tried to think of some joke to make. But a second later he had a new disquiet. Not one word had Ignatius spoken. It was not the half-breed boy. It was someone waiting to ambush him, and, unfooled by the silhouette—still waiting.

He knew then it was Garside. No explanation. He *knew*. He knew that the time—long anticipated, delayed, feared—had arrived. With a chill he felt it tingle down his body, and strangely, without the fear he expected. He knew it almost with relief, and with singular clarity of mind.

He let his hat and coat fall. He noticed the little fact of how they plopped on the ground, and he wondered what Abel would think. There were two of them, after all—Garside and Abel. He knew quite well that Garside did nothing without backing, without everything planned, flawless. Hence it was strange he would be in the cache house himself. Yet he was there.

He still thought Garside intended to shoot him. So the blow was a surprise. He had time to flinch, and the iron struck like an explosion in his brain. The whole left side

212

of his body seemed dead. He let go with his right hand. His left hand and arm, still holding, jerked like a hangman's rope. He fell to the ground. He was on his back. He reached for the gun which was not there. Desperately he kept grabbing for it.

"Gun, gun! He got a gun, Mist' Major!" cried Abel.

Garside was on the ledge, silhouetted by the stars. He leaped. McCoy saw his legs set stiffly out to land in his abdomen. He managed to turn half-over. He took a smashing blow, partially carried on his hip bone. He got up far enough to dive under the house. He strove for a moment, even a second, to make his stunned muscles function.

He made it to his feet. His shoulder rammed a brace timber. He crawled and rolled to the other side of it. Garside had a metal bar in his hands. He could see its shine. He fell back. The brace timber was between them. The bar made a clang as it struck wood. It flew from Garside's hands. He hunted for it across the ground.

McCoy then sprang for him. He tried to boot him in the head. He found instead the soft part of his body. Bracing himself with the timbers he came down with both heels in Garside's groin.

Their predicaments were now reversed. Now it was Garside who needed the fragment of time. He managed to roll over and draw his gun. He lay on his back, sensing rather than seeing the form over him, his gun against his side and his elbow on the ground, and he pulled the trigger.

As the gun exploded it occurred to Garside that the noise of a shot was the thing he had wished to avoid. But too late. The powder-flame gave him an instant impression of the hut, braces, timbers, but not McCoy.

He had hit nothing. Only the thud of embedded lead in the floor above. He turned and fired again. Then he groped for the iron bar.

He fell, and his fingers touched it. It was a chance in a thousand. Suddenly punishment didn't matter, he only needed to rise and finish. He got to his feet and took a step before turning. Then he saw the figure, the head, and holding the bar in both hands against the chance of again losing it, he swung.

He swung with all the savage power of his body. It was a horizontal blow and he felt the bone-smashing impact as the iron went through skull. He had the feeling of triumph, a transcendent, victorious, wild-elk sensation. Something older than man, deep in the heritage of animals, the survival of the fittest. He was glad then he had sent no one else, that he had come to do this job himself.

The man was driven against a brace bar, senseless, on his knees, and Garside, his fury victoriously unleashed, could not stop. He sprang on him and beat him again and again, battering the hated thing to pieces, smashing and crushing. "You son-of-a-bitch!" he whispered. "You son-of-a-bitch! Get in my way will you, you son-of-a-bitch! Get between her legs will you? You son-of-a-bitch . . ."

He checked himself. Reeling and exhausted, he filled his lungs like bellows. He leaned against a post briefly. A thought came to him that someone would be coming to investigate the shots. He had to get the body away. Killing was only the first half. He had to get him to the big hut to be discovered. After Dennis got them to battling. *If* he did. He turned away from the body.

"Abel!" Good, faithful Abel! "Abel! Where . . ."

In front of him was the figure of McCoy. Moonlit, a

tall shadow, but McCoy. He had the desperate impression that McCoy had risen from the dead. He tried again to lift the iron bar but his reactions were too slow and he was knocked to the ground. He stood and went down again. He struck against a broken brace timber and a gutting pain tore him. He got up, holding his abdomen. He felt as if his muscles had been severed so only parts of his body would operate. He reeled away. Men were shouting. He tripped over something solid and soft. It was human. It was Abel Tunis. He had a vague starlit impression of him. His neck was a headless stump. He had killed Tunis. Tunis had tried to help. The busybody. The ingratiating fool. Why did he think Garside needed his help?

He got to his feet. The stockade was in front of him. There was a great deal of shouting. He was wounded, so now they would be on him like hounds. He held his abdomen and retreated through the stockade where some posts had been taken out for firewood. There was a moon moving among broken clouds. His hand was slick. He looked and saw the dark glisten of blood. Blood was a black slick across his belt and down the left leg of his pants. He opened his shirt and saw open flesh. The timber had cut him like a dull knife. It was ripped jagged and deep. He had to hold his intestines in, but they were not severed. He needed time, time . . . Denker's! Denker would hide him because it was to his advantage, being involved in Garden City. And Pet.

He ran for a while, pinching his abdominal wall together. He slowed and had the sensation of walking in circles. The prairie seemed to be an endless cone making him walk in circles because one leg was not shorter than the other. It was a ridiculous sensation and he wanted to laugh about it. He was like a drunken man, and he kept walking. People seemed to be talking to him, voices in the top of his head. Cheers for Garside! Garside in full-dress uniform riding at the head of a parade. People were cheering and throwing money and roses. He stopped to get his bearings and looked back at the fort.

There were lanterns in movement. Crazy points of moving light like swamp fire. All he had to do to reach Denker's shanties was walk down the coulee. The coulee was a gentle swale, with here and there a cutbank that rose gray through the remnants of snow. Snow was a foot deep with an icy crust on the bottom, and he kept straying from the trail and falling. Then he smelled horse stables, and woodsmoke.

"Stop where you are!" It was Denker.

"Garside!" he said, snapping awake.

"So it is."

Denker had a double-pistol in his hand. He kept it there. He was a massive, dark lump of a man in the shadows.

"Keep clear!" he said when Garside started toward him. "Keep your hands clear."

"I'm unarmed. Unarmed. Denker . . ."

"What's the ruckus back there? What you on the lope for?"

"I'll tell you after awhile. I got cut up a little. I need some help. I want to stay here a couple of days."

"Who did it?"

"McCoy."

He laughed. It seemed to please him. He rolled his chew and spit. He watched Garside with his small, shrewd eyes. And he held the pistol.

"So, and now you come running. You, which was so high and mighty!"

He intends to kill me, thought Garside. His lightheadedness had vanished under the impact of necessity. His mind raced, planning and discarding, thinking what is this man? What does he want most? . . . Revenge? Money? His daughter's honor?

"You have to save me, Denker. Otherwise nobody will get to Garden City. And there goes your townsite. Without me they'll quit you cold. You'll be right back where you were. A squawman caging drinks. Everyone laughing at you."

He started to walk, walk steadily toward the double-gun which was big as a sawed-off shotgun, which *was* a sawed-off shotgun equipped with an old horse-pistol grip. But he stopped when Denker jerked the pistol to aim.

"No. You're finished. Finished or you wouldn't run."

"I need to be sewed up, that's all. Denker, I'll split with you. Half of all I have. They never butchered a mule of mine. Only lost four horses. My wagons alone are worth a small fortune in the camps. *Half*, Denker! Half to you!"

"That's good, but not good enough. Because I can pull this trigger and get it all. As guardian of Pet, the girl who is carrying your kid, your only heir. And that's *legal!* Hold up, now stand like a man, Garside, because I got to kill you."

"No! Denker . . ."

He pulled the trigger. The gun drove lead, flame, and coarse pellets of burning powder. The shot struck Garside with a noise like hail striking a hide tepee. The charge lifted him up on his toes as he came forward. He did not go down. He kept coming with his hands out as if to dive and grab the pistol, when close enough. Denker stood solid and waited for him. He waited until

217

Garside's stumbling charge had carried him to a distance of about ten feet, and pulled the second trigger. This charge seemed to break him in half. He fell and lay still.

Denker, after a while, put a toe under him and joggled him. Satisfied with his limpness, he heaved a sigh, and blew the fire out of the barrels before proceeding to reload.

"Pa, Pa!" Pet was calling.

"Stay back! Stay back, Pet!"

But the half-breed girl, growing front-heavy with child, came on, running past the corrals and some spreading twigs-white-in-the-moon box elder trees.

"What is it, Pa?"

"Well," he said reluctantly, "It's Garside."

"You killed him? Why, why?"

"No, I didn't. No! It was just that I had to put him out of his misery. It wasn't killing. Not really. He was knife-cut almost in half. His guts were hanging out. I'd have done the same thing for a horse."

She ran past and hurled herself on Garside. She pulled him with all her strength and rolled him on his back. The moon shone on his face.

"I had to do it, Pet. The poor devil. It was a mercy. I wouldn't let them get hold of him and hang him. It was what he asked me to do. He *asked* me to do it, Pet. He said, 'Shoot me. If you're my friend, shoot me.' So I shot him."

She waited and rocked back and forth. She ripped open the braids in her hair, and tore shreds out by the roots. She raked her face and neck with her fingernails until the blood flowed.

"You go right ahead, Pet. That's a widow's right. And don't let 'em claim you're not his widow. You are, and you got the build to prove it. Yes, by God, *you're his widow!* Don't you let 'em take the body away. I'll back you up in that. It's your legal right to claim that body—and *everything*."

The wagon train came down from Fort Hunter, spreading out to hunt for the new spring grass which grew bright green along the wet of snowbanks, and avoiding the Army road where ruts held ice and mud. Turning west at the Yellowstone it made numerous coulee crossings, each of them a day's accomplishment, and was stopped by a bank-full river pouring down from the south. After three days of trial and failure a raft ferry was constructed and the stream crossed. Once over, Denker pronounced the route clear sailing to Yellowstone City, and rode off to consult with the U.S. Commissioner about his daughter's claim to Garside's outfit.

He did not object that Doc Tiller had taken charge of his daughter—"The Widow" as he made a point of calling her. Doc had been with the girl almost constantly since leaving the fort and there were many jokes, out of his hearing, about his intention to share her inheritance. The fact was, as Aldo Rimmel pointed out, Doc had been enamored of the girl ever since Wyoming. He had spoken to Reverend Klinkke about marrying her, but Klinkke, pointing out the girl's papist leanings, had refused. Later, Doc had mentioned the matter to Elder Hulbush.

For Hulbush was still alive. On leaving the fort he had risen from bed to spend an hour or two each day in the seat of a wagon. From the Yellowstone onward he claimed himself well enough for a turn at the driving. But on reaching Yellowstone City, he went to bed trembling and with fever. A druggist from Minnesota, filling in as camp doctor, came and prescribed. His powders remained untouched as the old man lapsed into a coma. Then, near dawn on the second day, he opened his eyes and spoke to Bethel who came to stand over him.

"Where are we?" he said. "Is Manasseh back yet?"

"Not yet, Papa."

Manessah—the son who had never written after going off to war. The old man's mind had drifted back to a happier time, and he thought Manessah was still at home, gone to the town, or to a neighbors, for he said, "Tell him to take the harrow back. Samuel will be wanting it."

"Yes, papa," she said, and he died.

"He spoke to you?" asked McCoy when they stood together outside.

She nodded.

"Did he ask your promise for Garden City?"

"No, he thought we were back home and Manessah was there. I'm all right. Don't comfort me. I have faith that his leaving is also a beginning."

The train had already started to scatter. Six of the outfits were camped a quarter-mile away, getting ready to roll along the river southwestward to the new diggings at Emigrant City, and one of the outfits was Crandall's, a Gileadean. At least four more Gileadean families were preparing to head for the Bridger Ferry and the trail to Golden Cycle, a hardrock camp on the way to Last Chance; Brother Siles had fallen in with the Rimmels, enlisting more wagons for Rocker Creek, beyond the Three Forks. Only a few of the older people still had thoughts of Garden City.

"You know, your father was right?" said McCoy. "About Garside being the only one to lead you? He held you people together, and once he died you fell apart like a hoopless barrel."

She closed her ears to the mention of Garside, and did not wish to hear his name or think of him again, ever. She stood hand in hand with her husband. She stood very still, as one listening, but her eyes were closed. Several times she had felt a stir of life inside her. Now she was certain.

"What is it?" he asked, noticing the rapt smile on her face.

She told him, and they stood watching the west where the dawn's light grew and reflected back from the rimrocks, and from the bright endless road they would travel tomorrow.

We hope that you enjoyed reading this Sagebrush Large Print Western. If you would like to read more Sagebrush titles, ask your librarian or contact the Publishers:

United States and Canada

Thomas T. Beeler, *Publisher*
Post Office Box 659
Hampton Falls, New Hampshire 03844-0659
(800) 818-7574

United Kingdom, Eire, and
the Republic of South Africa

Isis Publishing Ltd
7 Centremead
Osney Mead
Oxford OX2 0ES England
(01865) 250333

Australia and New Zealand

Bolinda Publishing Pty. Ltd.
17 Mohr Street
Tullamarine, 3043, Victoria, Australia
(016103) 9338 0666